TEN-SPEED SUMMER

I never heard a sound behind me. But suddenly, out of nowhere, a pair of arms seized me.

"No use trying to get away! I've got you now!"

"Matt!" I knew his voice even before I recognized the familiar tall, slim figure, the green eyes laughing down at me.

"Who'd you think I was?" he asked. "Were you really scared?"

"Of course I was! What did you expect, coming at me like that! You want to give me a heart attack?"

My heart was thudding uncontrollably now, as though it would burst through my ribs. It raced even more wildly when Matt's arm tightened again as he gently drew me toward him. His face bent down to mine, and our lips met.

Bantam Sweet Dreams Romances
Ask your bookseller for the books you have missed

Ten-Speed Summer

Deborah Kent

BANTAM BOOKS

TORONTO · NEW YORK · LONDON · SYDNEY · AUCKLAND

RL 6, IL age 11 and up

TEN-SPEED SUMMER

A Bantam Book / January 1985

Sweet Dreams and its associated logo are registered trademarks of Bantam Books, Inc. Registered in U.S. Patent and Trademark Office and elsewhere.

Cover photo by Pat Hill

ISBN 0-553-24387-X

Published simultaneously in the United States and Canada

Bantam Books are published by Bantam Books, Inc. Its trademark, consisting of the words "Bantam Books" and the portrayal of a rooster, is Registered in U.S. Patent and Trademark Office and in other countries. Marca Registrada. Bantam Books, Inc., 666 Fifth Avenue, New York, New York 10103.

PRINTED IN THE UNITED STATES OF AMERICA

O   0 9 8 7 6 5 4 3 2 1

Ten-Speed Summer

Chapter One

"Your trip leader will meet you at the Albuquerque airport," the color brochure from North American Hostel Tours had assured me. But as I entered the waiting lounge, no one hurried forward to greet me. To my left, two little girls shouted, "Daddy! Daddy!" and danced around their beaming father. To my right, laughing and crying at once, an old woman embraced a young man in a three-piece suit. I stood alone, with the joyful sounds of reunion all around me.

I hadn't really felt lonely on the plane. I'd talked for a while to the woman next to me and read a short story in *Seventeen.* As we drew closer to Albuquerque, I turned again and again to my window to gaze down at the rugged mountains below. Even my nervousness about the summer began to fade as I saw that wild country for the first time, so different from the flat farmland of Illinois. This was the Southwest— and I would be exploring it in the weeks ahead.

During the flight Bruce's face surfaced in my thoughts every few minutes. I could hear his voice as plainly as if he were right beside me. "You'll be able to call me," he'd reminded me again that morning. "And we'll write. It's not the end of the world. You'll only be gone less than a month."

That was Bruce, always practical and optimistic. But it was easy for him to be optimistic. He could stay home in Kankakee, working in his father's hardware store. He could spend his evenings with our friends, hanging out in the park or at the burger joint. He wasn't the one who was going to spend the summer with a bunch of total strangers.

The lounge emptied rapidly as more and more friends and relatives were claimed. A balding man in a business suit asked me if I needed any help. He turned away when I said I was meeting someone, but I was feeling more conspicuous every moment. Where in the world was the trip leader? I didn't even know what sort of person I was supposed to be looking for.

Well, Mom had always insisted the challenge of being on my own was important. But what was I supposed to do in a strange airport in a strange city, twelve hundred miles from anyone I knew? Maybe I ought to turn myself in at the lost and found!

The brochure really hadn't spelled out where the trip leader would meet me, but the lounge by the gate where I got off the plane had certainly seemed the most likely spot. Still, maybe I was waiting in the wrong place. I decided to collect my luggage. I might even find the trip leader on the way, and I could always double back to check the lounge again.

I felt better as soon as I started walking. A sign directed me down a long corridor, and in another minute an escalator carried me smoothly to the lower level. All sorts of people hurried past: a man with a little boy perched on his shoulders, a woman with a yapping poodle in a carrier, two laughing girls with violin cases. It would be fascinating to sit in the airport with my sketch pad, trying to capture a bit of this movement and variety. Why had all these people flown to Albuquerque, New Mexico, that very day? Where had they come from? Did they wonder the same things about me?

I spotted my canvas saddlebags almost at once and lifted them from the revolving luggage belt. A few moments later the big cardboard carton that held my bicycle slid down the chute. The identification stickers Dad had glued on that morning were still plastered to its side. The box swung toward me, then rotated away again while I watched helplessly. How would I ever handle it alone? Even if I could wrestle it off the belt and hoist it onto one of those flat pushcarts, how would I get it back up to the passenger lounge? I couldn't take the escalator that had brought me down there. Mom might consider this a glorious challenge, but I wasn't sure I could meet it entirely on my own.

"Hi, Rhonda. Want me to help you with that?"

I straightened up with a jerk and whirled around. A tall, slender boy grinned down at me. "Your name's all over that box," he said in answer to my startled look. "You're going on the bicycle trip. I remember your name from that list they sent us. But even if I hadn't remembered, what else could you have in there but a bike?"

The boy was about my own age, almost seventeen, or maybe a year older. But he seemed so confident, as if nothing could be more natural than wandering on his own in a bustling airport. He couldn't be the trip leader I was looking for, could he?

"Are you taking the trip, too?" I asked as he grabbed the carton with my bicycle and set it down on the floor beside me.

"I sure am." He gestured toward a cart already loaded with saddlebags, a guitar in a canvas case, and a carton like my own. I stepped a little closer and read his name from one of the labels: "Matthew Jordon." The address was in Seattle, Washington.

"Thanks, Matthew," I said, giggling a little nervously. "Where are we supposed to go now, anyway? Do you know?"

Even if he wasn't the leader, I had the feeling he would know just what to do. And sure enough, he didn't disappoint me. "There's room for your bike on my cart," he told me. "The elevators are down there. By the time we get upstairs again, I bet somebody will be hunting for us."

He was taller and thinner than Bruce, but he showed a wiry strength as he lifted my bike onto the cart. His sparkling green eyes seemed to dart everywhere as we hurried down the hall. It was as if he didn't want to miss anything that might be happening around us. But when we reached the bank of elevators, he turned and studied my face. "You can call me Matt," he said. "Nobody calls me Matthew but my mother, and then it usually means I'm in trouble."

"OK, Matt," I said. "I'm just Rhonda. I never had any kind of nickname."

Matt nodded. "No, I guess you wouldn't," he said. "You look like the serious type. You're maybe a little bit formal, even. I bet you read a lot. You spend a lot of time studying. And you ordinarily wear jeans only about twenty percent of the time, right?"

I stared at him in astonishment. Was that really an accurate portrait of me? I did read a lot and devoted a lot of time to my schoolwork. But, "Twenty percent of the time?" I repeated. "How do you figure that?"

The elevator doors slid open, and Matt rolled the pushcart aboard. "Oh, that's just a figure off the top of my head," he said. "Before the start of a trip I like to look over the names of the people and picture what they might be like. Then when I meet them, I find out whether I was right."

"You've been on these trips before?" I asked as the elevator carried us back to the upper level.

"This is my third one with NAHT," Matt said. He pushed the cart through the door, and we walked back down the corridor to the passenger lounge. "Last summer I took a canoeing trip in Wisconsin, and two years ago I went on a bicycle trip, something like this one, only in the Canadian Rockies."

No wonder he was so self-assured. "You must really like them to keep coming back," I said.

"Each one is different. It all depends on the people you're with—oh, look—I think that's our leader over there."

A petite young woman in jeans walked toward us, waving frantically, her long brown ponytail bouncing with every step. "Hi!" she called. "You're with NAHT, right? I'm Mary Kay Martin."

"Rhonda McFarland. I waited for you up here, and then—" I began.

"We found each other down by the luggage," Matt interrupted. "Rhonda was getting her bike off the rack. Oh, my name's Matt—Matt Jordon."

"I'm sorry I'm late, but I had to meet two other kids, a guy off a flight from New York and a girl from . . ." Mary Kay tried to explain, but in the flurry of questions and answers I could hardly keep track of anything that was being said. It was enough to know that I had been found at last. It hadn't been so hard to meet the first challenge or two. But what else lay ahead?

"My van's parked out around back," Mary Kay said when the excitement began to ebb a little. "Calvin and Elise are waiting out there already."

"Elise Fournier," Matt mused aloud. "And Calvin Dexter the Third. I wonder what he'll be like."

He really *had* studied that list. Elise's name was barely familiar to me, but even I had found myself wondering what it would be like to meet someone named Calvin Dexter the Third. I was about to find out.

Mary Kay led the way out to the van and slid open the rear door. A couple of bags had already been stowed inside, and two bicycle cartons stood on the ground, waiting to be hoisted onto the roof. A slim, blond girl peered out of the van. As Matt, Mary Kay, and I maneuvered our bikes off the pushcart and started to set them on top of the van, the boy in the backseat called, "They're not all going to fit that way. Better turn that one at a ninety-degree angle. No, don't try to lay them flat; they'll never make it."

I glanced at him, a little annoyed. "You want to show us what you mean?" Matt asked smoothly.

The boy stepped out and stood for a moment, watching as we worked. "There, you're getting it now," he informed us. "See, that's the way I meant."

Somehow I was used to comparing every boy I met with Bruce. Calvin was about the same height as Bruce, but thinner, with a pasty complexion and large, horn-rimmed glasses. I turned to Matt, and in a flash we exchanged a meaningful look. What else could you expect from someone named Calvin Dexter the Third?

I scrambled into the van as Matt tied the boxes to the roof rack with a series of expert knots. "Hi," I said, smiling at the girl, "I'm Rhonda McFarland."

"Hi—Elise Fournier," she said, holding out a small, delicate hand. Elise was the only one of us who wasn't wearing jeans. She had on a frilly white blouse and a pair of dark dress slacks that looked as if they would show every speck of dust. The brochure from North American Hostel Tours had stressed that our clothing should be simple and practical, that there would be no need or opportunity to dress up. Just looking at Elise made me feel more prepared for the trip.

Then, as we entered the traffic and headed for the youth hostel outside Santa Fe, Bruce rushed into my thoughts again, and I choked back a surge of homesickness. Matt, Mary Kay, Elise, and Calvin commented on the mountains that loomed over Albuquerque, but I sat quietly, composing the opening lines of my first letter to Bruce. "I miss you already. If you were here, I think I could really enjoy this trip. You wouldn't believe the scenery. The mountains and valleys are beautiful. I'm going to send you some landscape drawings. The people I've met so far are OK, but if I had my choice, I'd still be back in Kankakee with you."

Chapter Two

"The first thing you'll learn about hosteling is that everybody's got to pitch in and help," Mary Kay said. "So right now I need volunteers for cooking supper and cleaning up afterward."

Elise smothered a groan and glanced at me across the living room of the hostel as though she hoped I would frown in sympathy. Calvin put his feet up on a brown leather footstool and turned a page in the book he was reading. I wanted to avoid being teamed up with either of them if I could, I decided. Neither one looked very enthusiastic about getting their hands dirty. The only member of the group who seemed willing to help out was Matt.

Sure enough, he was the first to answer the call of duty. "I'll cook tonight," he announced. "I'm starving."

"I'll help," I said quickly, before anyone else could offer.

Elise leaned back on the couch. "Well, I guess that means I can relax for a while," she said. "Hasn't this place got a TV?"

Mary Kay shook her head. "No, but some of the hostels do. You won't be deprived all summer."

"When's the rest of the group getting here?" Calvin asked, lowering his book a little. "There are four more people, according to the list of names we were given."

"They'll be coming in tonight," Mary Kay told him. "I've got to pick up Tony Nacotti at the train station later. The other boy, Clarke Dawson, said he'd be arriving by car."

"All the way from San Diego, by car?" Calvin asked. He consulted his copy of the list of group members to confirm Clarke Dawson's address.

Mary Kay shrugged. "All I'm telling you is what he wrote to us."

"What about the two girls, Phyllis Sanchez and Corinna Brown?" Matt asked. "They're both from around Santa Fe. You'd think they'd be the first ones here."

"They'll be here any time now. One of them, Corinna, is a Hopi Indian." Mary Kay hesitated. "I guess I ought to tell you now, so you won't be too shocked later. They're both students at the New Mexico School for the Deaf here in Santa Fe. Phyllis has some hearing, and she's supposed to speak and read lips pretty well. Corinna just uses sign language."

Deaf! It was almost too much for me to take in. The challenge of talking to strangers who could hear me perfectly well was difficult enough. But how would I communicate with deaf people?

I was relieved when Matt stood up and said, "Well, that'll be interesting. Come on, Rhonda, let's get started in the mess hall." His calmness reassured me.

The NAHT literature stated that almost any good-sized building could be converted into a youth hostel where travelers could spend the night inexpensively. This one, nestled in a little valley eight miles outside Santa Fe, was an old Spanish-style house of pink adobe brick. According to Calvin, who seemed to be an authority on virtually everything, the Pueblo Indians had been making bricks like these for more than a thousand years. Matt and I had to cross an open patio dappled by waning sunlight to step down into the kitchen. A counter covered with ceramic tiles ran the length of one wall.

Mrs. Gonzalez, the housemother who had taken us on a brief tour of the hostel when we arrived, emerged from the pantry at the back. "You can use anything you find in these cupboards," she told us. "All the pots and pans you'll need are either hanging on the wall or under the sink. And there's a big package of ground beef in the refrigerator—your leader stocked up for you."

"You can really tell we're in the Southwest." Matt pointed to a string of dried peppers hanging from a beam. "I think those are genuine chilies."

"It's a little complicated to fry them up if you're not used to it," Mrs. Gonzalez warned. "But there's chili sauce on the spice shelf, if you want to experiment with that."

Matt opened the refrigerator and brought out a clump of ground beef that looked big enough to feed a platoon. "We won't need all this," he said. "There are only five of us so far, maybe a couple more by dinner. What do you say we make chili burgers?"

"Sure, if you know how to make them," I said.

"Well, like Mrs. Gonzalez says, we can experiment."

Bruce was helpless in the kitchen, and he was almost proud of it. But Matt was clearly in command, and I stepped into the role of assistant chef. He got out garlic, onions, and green peppers and slid them toward me along the counter. I hunted up a knife, found a cutting board beneath the sink, and set to work. Mrs. Gonzalez hovered over us for a few minutes, making occasional suggestions. But once Matt showed her we had everything under control, she disappeared across the patio.

"How did you decide to come all the way from Kankakee, Illinois, and go on this trip?" Matt asked, splashing some more chili sauce over the meat.

"My cousin Helen went on an NAHT trip last summer, and she really loved it," I said. "She's been talking about it all year."

"So that got you interested?"

I hesitated. "Well, not exactly. It got my mother interested, though."

"Your mother wanted to sign up?" Matt asked, laughing.

My eyes were beginning to sting. I looked down at the mound of sliced onion on the board in front of me. "She'd have loved to," I said. "But the next best thing was to send me."

"You didn't really want to go then?" Matt asked in surprise, wiping his hands on his jeans.

"Well, I would have, I guess. I probably would have thought it was a really neat idea if it wasn't

15

for my boyfriend. We didn't want to be apart for so long."

"How long have you been going together?"

"Three and a half years," I said. "Since the middle of eighth grade." Our time together had settled into a smooth, comfortable, almost predictable pattern. We'd have lunch together in the school cafeteria. Bruce would drive me home every afternoon, and we'd spend time together until dinner. On Saturday nights we'd get together with Jack and Sally or some of our other friends and play video games or go out for pizza. There was something safe and reassuring about our routine.

I wondered how much of this I should try to explain to Matt. He was practically a stranger after all. I'd only met him a few hours before. But he seemed so sincerely interested that I told him the whole story. "That's the real reason my mother wanted me to leave home this summer," I said. She keeps telling me I'm too young to get so involved with anyone, that I have to meet new people or something."

Matt nodded encouragingly, and I went on. "My folks want me to go away to college somewhere, maybe to the University of Michigan, where Mom went. Bruce is going to the University of Illinois, close to home, and I would just as soon go there, too. So finally they said that if I'd go off on this bike trip this summer, and if I still wanted to go to the U. of I. when I got back, we could talk about it."

"You think they'll let you go?" Matt asked.

"Well, I know them pretty well. When they say we'll talk about something, they'll usually come around in the end. So I figure it's worth it. And like Bruce says, it's only a month. It ought to go by pretty fast."

"It will," Matt assured me. "You'll be surprised."

That seemed easy enough for Matt to say. He had wanted to go hosteling. Unlike me, Matt wouldn't count the days and with a sigh of relief, cross each one off a calendar.

Just as Matt was putting the first chili burgers on the stove, a commotion broke out across the patio. "Sounds like some of the other people just got here," Matt said. "I'll keep my eye on the burgers, and you can go on a scouting expedition."

For a moment I hung back, suddenly shy. If only Matt would come with me! But he was busy cooking. And after all, I told myself, I had to meet these new people sooner or later. I might as well get it over with now.

Two girls stood in the middle of the living room, looking around excitedly. The taller one wore a bulging backpack. The other one, who was stocky with high cheekbones and thick black hair, set down her duffel bag and waved her hands in a strange, questioning gesture.

"Rhonda, this is Corinna," Mary Kay said, pointing toward the stocky one. Motioning to the girl with the pack, she went on, "And this is Phyllis."

Elise's mouth gaped open, and her eyes were big and round. Calvin tried to look nonchalant, but he kept glancing from Corinna to Phyllis and back again as though he couldn't quite grasp the reality of their deafness. I probably looked just as confused myself.

"How are we going to talk to each other?" Elise blurted out.

How could she say that, right in front of them? Even if they couldn't hear her, they would understand the look of dismay on her face. And Mary Kay had said that Phyllis, the tall one, knew how to read lips.

But how *was* I supposed to greet them, I thought desperately as Phyllis approached me with a shy smile. "Hi," she said, her voice low and husky. "What is your name?" There was a strange roughness to her words, not quite smooth at the edges. But at least I could understand her. I hadn't quite expected her to speak at all.

"Rhonda," I said.

"Rhon," Phyllis repeated. She giggled and gave it another try. *"Rhon-da!"*

"That's it," I said, smiling back. She turned to Corinna, and the fingers of her right hand flicked in a series of quick, supple signals. Corinna replied with another set of lightning gestures. They were talking, talking with their hands.

Elise beckoned me over to her. "You and I can sleep next to each other tonight, can't we?" she whispered. "If I'm with one of them, I wouldn't know what to do, you know?"

It seemed almost funny, to be whispering around deaf people. But then the situation struck me with full force. Elise was the only girl on this trip I'd be able to talk to. Sure, we could sleep next to each other in the big room upstairs that served as the girls' dormitory. We could even share a tent when we camped out. But I had the feeling that Elise and I didn't really have much in common.

Of course, it did seem that I could talk to Matt pretty easily. But I couldn't spend too much time with him. Bruce was the only boy I needed in my life.

A fresh wave of loneliness engulfed me. How would I ever survive the weeks ahead? I wasn't looking forward to Mom's challenge.

I raced back to the kitchen. "Those two new

girls are here, and they really are deaf. They use sign language and everything."

Matt flipped a sizzling burger. "I'll have to meet them as soon as these are done," he said. "Here, have a taste and let me know if the next batch needs more chili sauce."

With his spatula he lifted a burger from the pan and into a bun. I bit into it eagerly—and my mouth burst into flame. "It's spicy enough already," I gasped, lunging for a glass of water. "I don't think you should add any more."

"You're not used to eating hot food, I guess," Matt said. "There's this nice little Mexican place back in Seattle; they really got me hooked." He continued putting burgers into buns.

"Maybe I can get used to it," I said. After all, I didn't want to hurt his feelings. I was just about to take a second, more cautious bite, when Elise burst into the kitchen.

"Oh, great! Food!" she exclaimed. "I need something to bolster me up!" She snatched one of the chili burgers from the plate and took a big, greedy bite. I had a hard time not giggling when her face turned crimson.

"What are you trying to do, kill us?" she shrieked, shoving past me to get to the sink.

"Gee, it was only an experiment," Matt said, tasting for himself. "The trouble is, you can always add more, but you can't subtract it."

It was more of a dilemma than I cared to cope with just then. "I'm going out to make a phone call," I said. "It won't take too long."

"Go ahead," Matt said. "Bet I know who you're going to call."

"I bet you're right." I fished through my pockets for the change I had saved for this purpose. It was just before five on Sunday. The rates would be low.

I had spotted a pay phone just inside the front entrance to the hostel. It wasn't very private, but for the moment nobody was around to hear me. Bruce was never much of a talker over the phone, anyhow, so we probably wouldn't say anything too personal. But it sure would be good to hear his voice.

Since it was almost five o'clock in Santa Fe, it would be six o'clock back home. Bruce's family would just be finishing dinner, and he wouldn't have gone out yet. With impatient fingers I dialed the number I knew so well. There was a decisive click and then far away the ringing of a telephone. *His* phone.

"Bruce!" I cried. "It's me!"

"Rhonda?" His voice was full of pleasure. I could picture the smile that must be brightening his face. "Wow! I really didn't think you'd call right away on the first night."

"But so much has happened, and I've got to

tell you about everything," I said. "And—and you sound the same as ever."

I told him about wandering around the airport, about the two deaf girls, about the fiasco of the chili burgers. Bruce didn't have much to say, just that he'd spent the afternoon helping his father clean out the garage. Still, it was a relief to hear his voice and to know that he was waiting for me back home. When I finally hung up and returned to the group, I no longer felt quite so alone. Later that evening I called my parents, and that cheered me up, too.

Chapter Three

"What are you looking so bright and cheerful for?" Elise demanded. "It should be illegal at six-fifteen in the morning!"

I stifled a yawn and reached for a slice of toast. "I don't know what makes you think I look cheerful," I muttered. "I'm still half-asleep."

My yawn triggered a chain reaction in Calvin and Corinna. Phyllis rubbed her eyes and helped herself to a second cup of coffee. Tony Nacotti, who had arrived late the night before, stared at us bleary eyed and barely replied when Mary Kay offered a brisk "Good morning." He was a short, dark boy with wiry black hair, which bristled out in all directions.

Only Matt seemed wide awake and ready for the new day. "Did anybody catch the sunrise?" he asked, setting down his glass of orange juice. "It was really spectacular!"

What would a sunrise be like out here? I wondered. The morning light would have to pierce the mist hanging over the mountains. That would be a picture worth sending home to Bruce. If only I'd been awake to see it.

"I don't mean to rush anybody," Mary Kay said, "but don't forget the rule in the hostel is that everybody's got to be out by seven."

"It's a gruesome rule, that's all I can say," Elise grumbled.

Corinna helped me as I gathered up the remains of breakfast. I was in no mood to talk, so our silence was easy, even comfortable, as we washed the dishes and rinsed them and set them in the rack to dry. But I noticed that she wore a pencil stub and a little pad of paper tied to her belt. That would make it easier to communicate when we had something important to say to each other.

"Whatever happened to Clarke Dawson?" Matt asked suddenly.

Mary Kay frowned. "According to his letter, he was supposed to be in by ten o'clock last night. I called his house, but there's no answer there. I don't know what could have happened, unless he changed his mind about going on the trip."

"We can't just leave without him, can we?" Elise protested. I got the distinct impression that she wasn't really concerned about the fate of Clarke Dawson—she was hoping we could delay our departure so she could run back up to the dorm and burrow into bed again.

"He hasn't even called to leave a message," Mary Kay said. "We can't wait for him. If he calls or shows up here later, Mrs. Gonzalez can make arrangements for him to meet us tomorrow night at Bandelier."

The Bandelier National Monument was the first stop on our itinerary. We would camp that night in a canyon famous for its ancient Indian ruins.

Phyllis turned to Corinna, and their hands spoke in quick, darting questions and exclamations. They both looked inquiringly at Mary Kay. "He's lost?" Phyllis asked in her guttural voice. "That other boy?"

Mary Kay shook her head vehemently. "Not lost. He might come later," she said, framing her words with her lips. Both girls fastened their eyes to her face. Phyllis nodded and signed something to Corinna, who gave a merry little giggle. But how much did they really understand? When we sat around talking in the living room the night before or grumbling over breakfast, had they felt left out?

Elise trailed after me as I ran upstairs. I stuffed my comb and toothbrush into one of my saddlebags and hurried down to the front entrance. Most of the others were ahead of me, and Matt and Tony already had their bikes uncrated and loaded with their belongings. Matt passed me a scissors, and I cut my crate open. In another moment my ten-speed bicycle stood on the gravel driveway, gleaming and ready to go.

"Here, let me help you with that," Matt said as I strapped my saddlebags to either side of the rear fender.

"This looks like the simple part," I said, glancing uneasily at the stack of rattraps outside the front door. In those cagelike, oblong contraptions we would carry the larger camping items, the pup tents, the pots and pans, and the Coleman stove, all provided by NAHT. Mary Kay said there was one rattrap for each of us.

Matt showed me how to fasten the rattrap on top of my saddlebags. It really wasn't as hard as I'd expected. Elise insisted that she couldn't figure it out and wasn't satisfied until Matt put hers on for her. His own bike looked so precarious, with his guitar strapped on top of his rattrap, that I wondered if he'd be able to keep his balance. But Matt didn't seem worried. After all, I reminded myself, he had done this before.

"We have to decide who'll take the pots and pans and who'll take the stove," Mary Kay said when we had everything assembled at last. "We'll take turns, so everybody will have plenty of chances. But believe me, the extra weight isn't any fun."

"Which is heavier, the stove or the pots?" asked Tony. He was short and stocky, with broad shoulders and arms rippling with muscles.

"I think the pots and pans are worse," Mary Kay said. "But the stove is bad enough."

"I'll take the pots and pans, then," Tony announced. "I can use the workout."

"Better to get your turn over with, you mean," Mary Kay said as Tony packed the clattering pans into his rattrap. "We'll get onto the Old Santa Fe Trail and take it all the way into town. That'll give you a chance to see the plaza in broad daylight."

I swung my leg over the bar and stood poised, my right foot on the pedal, my left foot ready to shove off from the ground. Tony Nacotti was already pedaling up the drive when Matt called after him, "Hey, this is the beginning of the whole trip! Let's all start off together."

Tony put his feet down and looked back, puzzled.

"You mean you want some kind of rite of passage?" Calvin asked. "Something to make it more ceremonious?"

"How about a bottle of champagne?" Tony said, smirking. "I'll smash it over my front fender."

"Hear ye, hear ye!" Mary Kay held up her hand for silence. "On this momentous occasion, this Monday, the twenty-fourth of June, we shall all set forth with a mighty burst of speed on the count of three." She paused to let her words sink in, holding a restraining hand toward Phyllis and Corinna, who watched her intently. "One!" she intoned, holding up a finger. "Two!" Another finger uncurled. *"Three!"*

"We're off!" Tony cried. And Elise sang, " 'We're off to see the Wizard, the wonderful Wizard of Oz.' "

I gave a push with my foot and started pedaling frantically, half-afraid I would skid on the gravel that crunched under my tires. Slowly at first, but gathering speed, we glided down the driveway and out onto the rutted road that led to the Old Santa Fe Trail, eight of us on bicycles, all together.

The Old Santa Fe Trail was actually a dirt road leading into town. A pickup truck rumbled past, and the driver waved and shouted a greeting I couldn't hear over the roar of his engine. Mountains loomed over us on our right, their peaks still hidden behind the early morning fog. Our wheels churned up a cloud of dust that swirled behind us. I could almost imagine the days long ago when wagon trains and cowboys on sweat-flecked horses had driven over the Santa Fe Trail through the wild mountains.

The road grew steeper and steeper. Our tight formation stretched into a wavering, ragged line. Mary Kay held the lead, with Tony right behind her. Matt pedaled smoothly ahead of me, and no matter how I puffed and struggled, I couldn't catch up.

In a way I was glad to be moving slowly. The low, prickly brush along the roadside, bursting here and there with flowers, was nothing like the green fields back home. Now and then we passed a big spiky cactus, and once Mary Kay called in delight, "Our first tumbleweed!" as a big green sphere spun toward me down the hill.

Gradually the city of Santa Fe closed in around us. First there were only scattered houses on either side of the road, and now and then a few small stores. Then the houses cropped up more and more frequently. Some were pink and some tan, but they were all built of the same adobe as the hostel. At last, after two hours of pedaling, Mary Kay signaled us to a halt beside the plaza.

The plaza reminded me of the pictures of village squares I'd seen in magazine articles about Mexico. A row of wrought-iron benches stood on a grassy square crisscrossed by stone walkways. On one of the benches an old man with a wide-brimmed hat sat reading the morning paper. A man and woman posed beside a tree, their arms around each other's waists, while another man snapped their photograph. A score of charming little shops lined all four sides of the square, shaded in front by pillared porticos.

"Let's take a little break and look around," Mary Kay suggested. "Some of these shops are interesting, but they're touristy and overpriced. We'd better meet back on this corner in half an hour, though. We've got a long way to go today."

Our bicycles looked oddly out of place, standing in a little cluster on the plaza. After the long ride, it was a relief to feel solid ground beneath my feet again. Elise sank onto a bench with a sigh. "I'll never make it," she moaned. "The summer is supposed to be for lying out on the beach, not for killing yourself like this!"

I was also tired, but we didn't have much time to rest. I wanted to look around before we had to mount our bicycles again.

I walked slowly around the plaza, peering

through shop windows at beaded moccasins, brightly colored pottery, and paintings by local artists. On the fourth side of the square, four Indian women had spread jewelry for sale on blankets on the sidewalk.

They sat on the ground, their skirts gathered around them, and barely moved as I approached. But I felt they were watching me as I bent to inspect their wares. "How much is this?" I asked, holding up a silver filigree bracelet.

The first woman eyed me carefully, as though she were sizing me up. "Twenty-five dollars," she said at last.

I didn't have much money to spare, and what little I had I wanted to save to buy a special present for Bruce. "It's awfully pretty," I said, setting it down on the blanket again. "But I really can't afford it."

I started toward the next blanket, but the woman's voice pulled me back. "Twenty dollars," she said. "You look like a nice girl to me. It's a special price just for you."

I gazed at her in amazement.

"I think you're supposed to bargain with her," whispered Matt, stepping behind me.

"Bargain? I thought that just happened in exotic places like Baghdad," I exclaimed. "This is the United States."

"Well, the Southwest can be pretty exotic," said Matt.

"Nineteen?" the Indian woman offered.

I shook my head. "I can't," I said. "I wish I could, though."

"That bracelet would look really great on you, I bet," Matt said.

"You really think so?" Why should Matt say a thing like that to me? Even after all these years, Bruce hardly noticed when I wore jewelry, and he knew me a lot better than Matt did.

"Come on, gang! Let's hit the road!" Mary Kay's voice broke into my thoughts. Together Matt and I crossed the plaza to the corner where our group was reassembling. Calvin, Phyllis, and Tony were there already. Phyllis showed me a bow-shaped enameled barrette she had bought.

"OK, where are the others?" Mary Kay asked. "I guess I can't blame Corinna for being late, she couldn't hear me calling. But what's Elise's excuse?"

"You can always count on Corinna being late," Phyllis said in her low voice.

It was Matt who finally made a quick survey of the shops and rounded them up. Mary Kay's half hour had stretched into forty-five minutes by the time we were ready at last.

"Now the really tough part starts," Tony said

with satisfaction. "Here's where we find out who's going to make it and who isn't."

"Let's go once around the plaza," Mary Kay said. "Then we'll head over to Saint Francis Drive and out of town."

She led the eight of us in a laughing parade as we swung in a farewell loop around the plaza. I waved to the Indian woman who had tried to sell me the bracelet, and she smiled back, calling, "Fifteen! I'll give it to you for fifteen!"

Then the plaza fell behind us, and we were all following Mary Kay into the shining summer morning.

Chapter Four

I woke to the chattering of birds the next morning. The sun was already burning away the dampness of the night air, but I felt stiff and creaky from sleeping on the ground. Wiggling out of the pup tent I had shared with Elise, I met the sharp, clean smell of fresh coffee. Matt and Phyllis, who had breakfast duty that morning, were already hard at work.

"There's a much more direct route from Santa Fe to Bandelier," grumbled Calvin, pulling a New Mexico road map out of his saddlebag to prove his point.

"Yes, but you wouldn't want to bike along it

with all the traffic," Mary Kay insisted. "There's a whole spider's web of back roads we'll take all the way up into Colorado to Boulder. It may not be as the crow flies, but we can avoid the highways, and it's a lot more scenic."

Once we turned onto the narrow dirt road even Calvin fell silent. The work of pedaling engrossed us all completely. Over the past two months I had practiced distance bicycling, just as the NAHT literature advised. But nothing in Kankakee, Illinois, could have prepared me for the rolling hills of this sprawling countryside. Again and again we panted our way to a hill's crest and coasted blissfully down the far side, only to begin the process all over again at the bottom. While we biked, an old children's song jingled through my head: *"The bear went over the mountain, the bear went over the mountain. . . ."*

"I'm getting saddle sore," whined Elise. She had dismounted and was wheeling her bike up the hill, sweat rolling down her forehead. "When do we take a break, anyway?"

"For lunch," I grunted. It was too much effort to say more. *"The bear went over the mountain, and what do you think he saw? He saw another mountain. . . ."*

But as I coasted downhill again, trying to summon my strength for the next assault, Matt shouted from up ahead, "Chow time! We're going to stop and buy food!"

Sure enough, a tiny town lay nestled in the valley below us. We pedaled down a dusty main street, past a barber shop, a bank, and a boarded-up restaurant, to stop at last in front of Suzie's Market.

"Just get things to make sandwiches with and something to drink," Mary Kay told us. "You don't want to have to drag around a ton of leftovers all afternoon. Before we get to Bandelier we'll buy food for supper."

The plump, red-faced woman behind the counter—Suzie herself, we supposed—stared in amazement as we swept up and down the two cluttered aisles like a swarm of locusts. My legs wobbled, my head felt light, and everything on the shelves, from the boxes of M&M's to the bags of potato chips, looked not only delicious but absolutely essential for survival.

"Let's take about four packages of this salami," said Tony, grabbing them as though he could devour them all in one bite.

Calvin made a wretching sound. "Salami! That stuff is full of chemicals. *You* can eat it if you want, but *I'm* not going to."

"Let's just buy *something*!" Elise broke in. "I'm going to faint if I don't eat soon!"

"We don't all have to eat the same thing," Matt

said logically. He took two packages of Tony's salami. "What else do people want? Tuna fish? Peanut butter and jelly? Some of these rolls?"

"Sounds good to me," I said, grinning at him. Matt might not be the world's best cook, but he had a way of bringing order out of confusion. Suzie was soon ringing up our purchases.

"Bandelier!" she exclaimed when Mary Kay told her our destination. "It's beautiful out there. You'd better watch it if you're camping out, though. They've got bears and cougars, too."

"Lions and tigers and bears!" Tony exclaimed, and Matt and I joined him in the little song from *The Wizard of Oz.* " 'Lions and tigers and bears, oh my! . . .' "

But deep down I was a bit afraid of the bears and cougars Suzie had mentioned. I tried to put the thought out of my mind. Suzie called a cheery goodbye as we straggled out the door.

We ate at a picnic table a quarter mile up the road. Nothing had to be cooked, so there was no need to unpack the pots and pans from Tony's bike. Mary Kay said we could take a whole hour to rest. As soon as I had eaten and helped to gather up the garbage, I dug one of my sketch pads out of my saddlebag and set to work on a drawing to send to Bruce.

The group scattered across the field on the

side of the road. Voices floated to me from far-ther and farther away. I lost track of time as I worked, swiftly penciling in the grassy hilltop where I sat, the trunk of a spreading pine, the rolling field dotted with bristly sagebrush. It was worth the aching in my legs just to be there, part of this landscape so unlike anything I'd ever seen before. If only Bruce could be there to share it all with me, instead of waiting for my letters back in Kankakee.

Suddenly a shadow dropped across my pad. I looked up, startled, hastily covering the half-finished sketch with my hands.

"I didn't mean to scare you," said Matt, kneeling down beside me. "I just wondered what you were doing, that's all."

"Oh, it's nothing much." Bruce always admired my pictures, simply because I had drawn them. But I didn't often show them to other people.

Still, just as I'd known he would, Matt asked, "Can I take a look at that?"

Reluctantly I handed him the pad. He studied it for a long, tense moment as though he were judging every detail. I don't know why my heart started pounding the way it did. After all, I hardly even knew Matt. His opinion shouldn't have mattered to me one way or the other.

But I felt a glow of relief and pleasure when he

handed the pad back to me with a nod of approval. "I like it," he said. "Not that I'm any expert on art, but you look like you know what you're doing. Do you take classes or anything like that?"

"I was in a life drawing class last winter. It was sponsored by the University of Illinois, and they only accepted ten high-school students, so I was really lucky to get in."

"It wasn't luck, it was talent," Matt stated.

My cheeks flushed, and I didn't know what to say. Fortunately, he didn't require an answer. "Don't let me interrupt you," he went on. "I'll just sit here. We've got fifteen more minutes, if you want to finish up."

He leaned against the trunk of the tree behind me so he wouldn't block my view. After a few uncertain seconds I picked up my pencils and tried to go back to work. I never found it easy to draw if I felt that anyone was peering over my shoulder, and even Bruce had learned to let me work by myself. At first I kept glancing back at Matt, wishing he would get up and go away. But in a few minutes the field and the cloudless sky and the line of mountains on the horizon began to work their spell again. I almost forgot that Matt was sitting there at all.

"Come on, troops!" Mary Kay called as I was adding the final touches. Already Tony and Phyllis waited beside their bikes. Calvin trotted across the field while Elise trailed forlornly after him.

Matt watched expectantly as I scrambled to my feet. I didn't wait for him to ask, but handed him the completed sketch. He turned it this way and that as we walked out to the road and joined the others.

"That's amazing," he said, handing it back to me at last. "You got so much into it. Even one of those great big crows that are flying around all the time."

"They're not crows, they're ravens," Calvin remarked. "Crows live at lower altitudes. They're smaller and—"

"Hey, let me see!" Elise broke in, snatching the picture out of my hand. "You never told me you're an artist!" She made it sound as if we'd known each other all our lives.

By now my sketch pad was passing from hand to hand, and everyone had a comment to make. Mary Kay said that if this scenery impressed me, she couldn't wait to see what I'd think of Bandelier. Calvin said I shouldn't be so representational, I should try to capture the spirit of the scene without so many little details. Phyllis tried to ask me something that I didn't quite understand the first time. She frowned and tried again more slowly. "Do you do paintings, too?"

"Yes," I said, nodding to make the point even clearer. "I didn't bring any canvases to work on, though. Too much stuff to lug around."

In a way it was fun, being the center of attention. Still, part of me wished that everyone hadn't seen my picture. It felt public now, as though each of them had claimed a little piece of it. I had meant it for Bruce alone.

I pushed those uneasy thoughts aside as Corinna dashed up, laughing and breathless, her hands full of purple wild flowers. She began to sign some eager, mysterious message to Phyllis, and the flowers fell gently to the ground at her feet. I didn't know what they were discussing, but their laughter was infectious.

"Well, everybody's here," said Mary Kay. "We've got a long haul this afternoon. Next stop is Bandelier."

Lunch must have given me a second wind because my pedaling seemed smoother and easier that afternoon. Even Elise stopped complaining and managed to keep up with everyone else. We rode between fields of corn and alfalfa, passed lonesome farmhouses, and once had to slow down while four big spotted cows ambled across the road.

"It'll start getting steeper from here on," Mary Kay warned us when we paused for apple juice and a rest toward four o'clock. "You'll think it's never going to end, but it's worth the effort, believe me!"

Tony burrowed in one of his saddlebags and extracted a Sony Walkman. "I need moral support if I've got to haul all this hardware," he muttered. "I don't know why we've got to have so many pots and pans."

At first I couldn't detect much of a difference in the road, and I assumed that Mary Kay had been exaggerating. But within twenty minutes the wheels of my bike began to turn more and more slowly. I shifted gears, and that helped for a while. But soon I rose from the seat, driving the pedals with my full weight. "This road just won't quit," Tony called. Each time I rounded another curve I dreamed it would be the last. But each time a new stretch of road lay in wait, daring me to struggle on.

Our orderly line of bicycles fell to pieces. Naturally, Elise was the first to dismount and walk, but moments later Phyllis and Calvin followed her example. I passed Tony, still pumping valiantly despite his cargo of cooking gear. Corinna pedaled beside me, her lips set in a fierce, determined line. Far up the road Mary Kay forged ahead. And a few yards in front of me, his back straight, his head held high, rode Matt.

This was one more of those challenges Mom had said were so wonderful. This was how I was supposed to test my limits and discover who I really was. Of course, I might discover that I was a corpse and end up in the brush by the side of the road, but no matter.

I glanced at Matt again. Tirelessly he drove his pedals, never looking back the way he had come. Somehow I knew that I, too, could will myself to go still farther.

We were approaching yet another bend in the road, and once more my hopes rose. Perhaps, at last, the end was in sight. But as Matt rounded the curve ahead of me, he uttered a groan of despair.

For an instant I wanted to give up right where I was. Anything that could make Matt groan like that had to be pretty awful. And what met my eyes, as I followed him around the turn, surpassed my wildest dread. Above us loomed a sheer mountain wall, stretching up endlessly toward the clouds. And the road climbed straight up that rock face, merciless and unrelenting.

"OK," Mary Kay told us. "This isn't an endurance contest or anything. You might as well all walk this last section."

The earth felt unsteady beneath my feet, but it was only the weary trembling of my legs. Matt leaned on his bike, panting, as Corinna and I caught up to him. "We'll make it," he promised. "It can't be as bad as it looks."

"I wouldn't bet on it," I gasped. And Corinna flung up one hand in an eloquent gesture of utter defeat.

But in a minute or two I caught my breath. We trudged on, wheeling our bikes beside us. The sun beat down on my shoulders, and the road grew steeper with every step.

"Look at these rock formations," called Calvin. "All those little holes like Swiss cheese—that's because when it was forming there were bubbles of gas trapped inside."

It was true. The rock wall that loomed above us was pitted with strange round cavities. But how could Calvin think of scientific explanations when I barely had the energy even to look up from the road? I could hardly manage to set one foot in front of the other, left, right, left, right.

Suddenly Mary Kay's voice rang out ahead, a shout of triumph. A thrill of excitement rippled through our straggling line. Somehow I found one final surge of strength to carry myself and my bicycle over one more mound of rock.

And then, miraculously, I rose above the final crest. Stunned, I gazed at the marvel below me, a deep, clean chasm sliced out of the earth, green with pines, crossed by a stream that shimmered like a silver ribbon. This was the goal that had drawn us up the mountain. This was Bandelier Canyon.

Chapter Five

"We'll do this from time to time throughout the trip," Mary Kay explained the next morning as she rinsed the frying pan in a bucket of water from Frijoles Creek. "You don't want every minute to be scheduled. It helps to break up the traveling with some time to yourself."

"You mean we should just wander off by ourselves?" Elise asked doubtfully. "There are so many crazy trails on the map. What if somebody gets lost?"

"Don't worry about a thing," Tony assured her. "I'll take you on a guided tour, OK?"

I couldn't understand why Elise had so much

trouble planning her day. I knew exactly what I wanted to do. I had wakened to a chorus of birds singing and crawled out of our pup tent while Elise was still asleep. I had made my way along the creek until I found a high flat rock that the sun had just begun to warm. There I sat, hardly breathing as I drank in the stillness of the crags around me, the glint of the tumbling water, the chatter of an unseen bird in the pine branches overhead. After breakfast, I resolved, I would come back and make a sketch that would capture it all for Bruce.

Tony dismissed my sketchbook with a shrug as I slipped it into my day pack. "That looks like a lot of unnecessary work to me," he remarked. "Why do you think they invented the camera?"

"This is different," I insisted. "When I draw something, it's more personal."

"Maybe," Tony said. "To me it just looks like work."

But nothing he said could discourage me. I found a pine-studded knoll with a good view of the canyon below and set to work. I wouldn't send all of my pictures to Bruce, I decided. I wanted to keep a few of them for myself, to remind me of the places I'd been. I'd work on some during the fall and winter, making them into full-scale paintings.

I was finishing up my second sketch when the

snap of a twig behind me made me whirl around. But it wasn't a bear, it was only Corinna. She held out a map of the canyon, which she'd picked up at the park office, and traced one of the trails with her index finger. She smiled invitingly and beckoned me to follow her.

"Sure. Why not?" I stopped short. What was the use of talking? Corinna hardly seemed able to read lips at all.

I smiled apologetically and offered a vigorous nod. Stuffing my sketch pad and pencils into my pack, I started after her along the trail.

It was wide and smooth at first, sloping gently downhill. There was something nice about walking instead of riding a bicycle. I felt closer to the earth, and we moved slowly enough to notice each new cluster of wild flowers and every patch of feathery moss. And all around us was the "Swiss cheese rock" that Calvin said had been formed by cooling bubbles of gas hundreds of thousands of years ago. As we made our descent into the canyon, a cliff rose on our right. It was pockmarked with holes, some of them no bigger than my fist, others so large that a child could have crawled inside.

Suddenly Corinna darted ahead, waving and pointing up the cliff face. Following her gaze, I spotted a hole even wider and deeper than the others. It wasn't merely a hole, it was a cave. And a narrow wooden ladder led up to its entrance, fifteen feet above.

Corinna pulled a pamphlet from her back pocket and flipped through its pages. I peered over her shoulder, and together we read the park's official explanation: "Natural caves in the canyon were once the homes of the Anasazi people, who lived here until about 1200 A.D. In some of Bandelier's caves, ancient drawings can still be observed."

"Let's go up there," I said, and this time I forgot to worry whether Corinna could read my lips. My meaning was plain enough. The ladder had been placed there by the park service so hikers could climb up to the cave, I supposed. But as I mounted I had the unsettling fear that if I leaned back too far I would throw the ladder off balance and be hurled to the ground. At last I pulled myself over the threshold and perched in the cave's mouth, grinning down at Corinna as she scrambled up to join me.

The cave was cool and dry, its stone floor littered with twigs and pine needles. The ceiling was so low that we had to bend almost double. At the far end of the room was the narrow entrance to a second chamber, hidden in darkness.

As Corinna's pamphlet had predicted, strange faces and figures were etched on the walls and ceiling. Corinna pointed to a rough animal drawing, the body almost blotted out by time. She cocked one hand beside her head like an ear, then drew whiskers in the air next to her cheeks.

"A cat!" I exclaimed. "No, it's got to be a wildcat—a cougar."

Corinna watched my face keenly. She was just offering me a pencil stub and a slip of paper from her pad when a scraping sound and a cascade of pebbles made me spin to face the dark opening at the back. My heart pounded. The image of a lean, sinewy beast flashed through my mind. I was sure fierce yellow eyes blazed at us through the gloom.

"Hi!" It was Matt's voice, and in another second his head appeared at the entrance to the cave's far room, his face lit by the glow of a match. He wriggled through the narrow opening and crouched on the floor beside us.

"You scared me!" My heart was still knocking out of control. "Why didn't you say something right away?"

"I wasn't so sure who *you* were, either," Matt admitted. "That room goes way back. I was in there, and I thought I heard something, so I kind of sneaked out to investigate."

Corinna scuttled off to explore the room Matt had just left. Was she thinking about other Indians, men and women who might have lived in this very cave long ago? I peered after her, but the thick darkness was uninviting.

"It's kind of eerie in here, isn't it?" Matt said, leaning back against the curving wall. "You get to thinking about the people who once lived here, and you wonder whether their spirits are still hovering around."

I thought back to the night I'd just spent in the pup tent, trying to curl into a comfortable position with rocks and tree roots jabbing my ribs. "Imagine sleeping on a stone floor every night," I said. "And the Anasazi didn't have down sleeping bags, that's for sure."

"You know what they used to do with those ladders?" Matt asked. "They'd pull them up inside the caves so their enemies couldn't get up to them. Calvin was telling me about it this morning."

Corinna emerged again, brushing a lock of hair back from her forehead. She sat for a few moments in the mouth of the cave, then, with a goodbye wave, vanished down the ladder.

I was about to follow her, then realized she might want to be alone for a few minutes.

Matt asked, "Do you want to see the rest of this place?"

Though I hadn't wanted to venture into the far room with Corinna, the idea sounded more inviting when it came from Matt. "OK," I said. "I wish I had a flashlight, though."

"I've still got plenty of matches," Matt said, striking one as he spoke. "Come on, it's kind of neat back there."

The ceiling of the far room was only about four feet from the floor. We crept along on our hands and knees. A narrow shelf of rock extended along the far wall. As I slid my hand along it, my fingers closed on something hard and waxy. The stub of a candle!

"Somebody's been up here since the Anasazi," Matt said, lighting it with a fresh match. The candle drove back the lurking shadows and filled our end of the room with a soft, warm glow. The cave felt cozy now, a place where we could sit and talk.

"How do you like the trip so far?" Matt asked, stretching out his feet.

"It's interesting," I said carefully. "I mean, I didn't expect it to be like this."

"Like what?"

"Well, for one thing, I hadn't thought much about the country we'd be seeing. And getting to know the other people in the group is kind of fun, like you said it would be. I guess I didn't think much about the trip beforehand. It was just something I had to get through before I could go back home."

"Back home to Bruce," Matt said, and I wondered whether I had imagined a note of wistfulness slipping into his voice. I glanced over at him, startled, but he smiled back unperturbed.

The world outside seemed very far away. No sound reached us through the stone ceiling. Maybe the Anasazi had the right idea, after all, I mused. A cave like this could be a peaceful little haven, secluded from all the bustle below.

But we couldn't stay there forever. Finally Matt broke the spell. "We'd better go out and find Corinna," he said at last. "I'm going to follow this trail all the way to the river, if you and Corinna want to come with me."

"Great." Carrying the candle in one hand, I crawled back the way we'd come. The first room seemed spacious and airy compared to the place where we had just been sitting. Sunlight streamed in through the entrance, and a gentle breeze brought us the clean scent of pine. A raven flapped past the cave entrance with a low, hoarse cry. As Corinna had done, I sat in the mouth of the cave, gazing down from my lordly perch.

Then I gasped in dismay. The ladder was gone!

It lay stretched on the ground, useless and out of reach.

"Oh, wow!" Matt groaned, peering out past my shoulder. "How could that have happened?"

"Corinna!" I shouted. *"Corinna,* where—" But what was the point? If she were ten feet away, she still couldn't have heard me.

"If I had a pole or something, I could try to lift it up," Matt said. "It'd be kind of hard, but—"

"But we haven't got a pole," I said. "This is unbelievable! They won't think to look for us till supper time." Not that it would be such a terrible way to spend the day, I reflected. We could sit here in the cave talking, eating the sandwiches I'd brought in my day pack. I had told Matt a lot about myself; maybe this was my chance to learn more about him.

"Well, don't worry," he said, patting my knee. "All is not lost. I can lower myself and drop down, it'd only be a few feet. And actually I think I see a couple of toeholds."

But before he could chart a course of action, Corinna popped up from a clump of bushes. She grinned at us impishly, and suddenly it all made sense. She had taken the ladder away herself, as a practical joke!

Still grinning, she raised the ladder into position again, then backed off, giggling, as I scrambled to the ground. "What a thing to do!" I cried. Even if she couldn't hear me, she knew what I was talking about. She tried to put on a look of wide-eyed innocence, but her face kept wrinkling with laughter.

"The Anasazi had the right idea," Matt said, shaking his head. "Next time we'd better pull the ladder up inside.

"Come on," he called, starting down the trail. "It's five miles to the river and back. We've got to get going."

We were all pretty quiet that night as we huddled around the campfire after supper. I'd never thought that five miles could be such an immensely long way. But the hike to the river at the canyon's floor had led us up and over jumbled piles of boulders. And the trip back was all uphill. When we staggered back into camp at four o'clock, we were just in time to gather firewood and prepare for the evening meal.

Elise lay sprawled on a blanket, too exhausted to move. "Where did you end up hiking to?" I asked her.

She raised her head and pointed an accusing finger at Tony. "It was his big idea," she said feebly. "He wanted to take this trail that's about five hundred miles long. There were supposed to be some old statues of mountain lions."

"It was your fault we didn't get to see anything," Tony reminded her. "You conked out about ten yards out of camp."

He put on his headphones and lost himself in the music from his Walkman. Elise turned away indignantly. "Matt," she asked, "when are you going to play your guitar for us?"

Matt put another log on the fire and straightened up. "You want me to?" he said eagerly. "Do you sing?"

Elise giggled. "About as well as one of those big crows," she said. "But you do, I bet."

Matt shrugged. But he went over to the pile of gear by his bicycle and gently lifted his guitar from its case. He sat on a dome-shaped rock, rested the guitar on his lap, and strummed the strings with his fingers. For a few minutes he became absorbed in tuning, testing each string again and again until he was satisfied with its pitch. He played a series of soft, rippling chords, and little by little they took shape, weaving gracefully into the opening of a song.

It was a quiet, thoughtful song about a man who lived like a miser, trying to be safe all the time and never really living. At the close of the song, he lay dying and knew his lifetime had been squandered away.

"Wow! That's fantastic!" Elise exclaimed before the final notes had faded. I just wanted to sit still for a few moments, to let the magic of the melody and of Matt's strong, low voice last as long as possible. But Elise couldn't be quiet. "Who wrote that?" she demanded. "Billy Joel? I never heard it before."

Matt hesitated. "I did," he said shyly.

"I sure envy talented people." Mary Kay sighed. "About the only thing I'm any good at is getting from point A to point B."

"That song really wasn't bad. You do some nice things with lyrics," Calvin said. It was the first time I'd ever heard Calvin praise anyone's accomplishments without reservations.

"It really was pretty," I said softly. I wasn't even sure Matt heard me. He was strumming again, and we all waited. Tony even removed his headphones. The song was familiar this time, though I didn't know all the words. Elise edged closer to Matt and hummed along on the refrain.

One song followed another. Matt played some that everybody knew and got us to sing along with him. But other times he played gentle, haunting tunes he had composed himself. I strained to catch every word, fascinated by each new glimpse into his thoughts and feelings.

Phyllis and Corinna had moved to the fringe of the group, their hands flashing in silent conversation. What did they think of all this—Matt's fingers darting up and down the neck of a guitar, our mouths opening in unison, our feet tapping and bodies swaying to some unknowable beat? After a while Calvin joined them. I could hear him talking, though I couldn't quite make out his words. The next time I glanced their way,

Phyllis was leaning toward him, her eyes watching his face intently.

By now Elise was almost sitting in Matt's lap, gazing up at him enthralled. Matt didn't seem to mind her admiration, either. He kept looking down at her as if his songs were meant for her alone.

Tony picked up a stick and snapped it in two. I could almost read his thoughts—he'd spent all day with Elise, and now she didn't even glance in his direction. She acted as if Matt were the only boy in the world.

But that shouldn't have bothered me. Sure, Matt and I were becoming friends, but if he and Elise decided they liked each other, what difference could that make to me? Bruce was the only boy I could ever care about.

Phyllis and Calvin got to their feet and walked a little way down the path of the camp. Corinna sat alone, bent over a sheet of paper. I slipped over to join her.

She lifted her hands and showed me what she'd been working on. She had drawn a caricature of Calvin, his head absurdly large and his mouth wide open. Beside him she had sketched a comical portrait of Phyllis, her huge round eyes hungry for every word.

"I didn't know you like to draw, too!" I exclaimed. "That's neat."

Corinna picked up her pen. "He likes her because she doesn't interrupt him," she wrote.

I giggled. It was true. In Phyllis, Calvin had found the ideal audience for his facts and theories—someone who would rarely argue and almost never interrupt.

But there was something I had to get straight. I took Corinna's pen and wrote, "What was the big idea stealing the ladder this morning?"

She grinned and began to scribble feverishly. At last she thrust her note into my hand. "Just thought you two might like to be alone," I read. "You did, didn't you?"

I turned away to hide the blush that crept up my cheeks. Now that I looked back on it, it *had* been fun sitting up there with Matt, trying to figure a way out of our predicament. But how had Corinna known that?

"Ha-ha. Very funny," I wrote to Corinna. But later, I tore her note into tiny pieces, and as I put them in the trash bag, I told myself I was putting Matt out of my mind for good.

Chapter Six

By Friday morning at a new campsite, I was starting to feel like an old hand at cooking over an open fire. Everything we did was hard work, from boiling our drinking water, to gathering firewood, to scrubbing our pans in an icy stream. But there was something wonderful now about looking up at the floating clouds as I stirred a panful of eggs, the fire's heat thawing the morning chill out of my bones.

"We're staying at Espanola tonight," Calvin remarked.

"Whose turn is it to carry the pots and pans?" Mary Kay asked brightly.

"Not mine," Tony said with satisfaction. "I've already done my bit."

"Let's get the phantom to carry them for us," Matt suggested. "Clarke Dawson ought to do something to earn his keep around here."

"I'll get my turn out of the way," Calvin volunteered. "It might not be too bad. Looks like it's going to be mostly downhill this morning."

Calvin was right. We left on a glorious downhill sweep, laughing and waving and calling to one another. The wind fanned my face and whipped my hair back. I wished I could sail on that wave forever, free from thoughts of the past or the future.

But, of course, it couldn't last. By midmorning we were back among the familiar rolling hills, and "the bear went over the mountain" jingled through my head once more as we pedaled up and over, up and over.

"At least we get to sleep in real beds tonight, with sheets and pillows and everything," Elise said when we stopped for our afternoon break. "I've had my limit."

"It'll be great to take a shower, that's for sure," I agreed, struggling to work some of the tangles out of my hair. Working with a pan of water from a stream just wasn't the same.

Corinna flopped down beside us, a peach in one hand, her pad and pencil in the other. She bit into the peach and pointed at Tony, shaking her head.

Usually Tony seemed to make up for his short stature by flinging himself into every task with twice as much energy as anyone else. But now he had stretched himself full-length in a patch of shade beside a tall rock. His face looked pale, and when Phyllis passed him to get a fresh cup of apple juice, he didn't even turn his head.

"After all his tough talk," I said, "he looks like he's giving up already." Corinna tore off a blank slip of paper and waited while I wrote out what I had said. Somehow, committed to print, it seemed too mean-spirited.

Mary Kay went over to Tony, her faced creased with concern. I couldn't hear what she said, but Tony sat up, mopping his forehead, and waved her away.

"He says he's fine," reported Matt, who had been near enough to overhear their conversation. "The thing is, he was bragging to me the other night that he never bothered to practice bicycling on weekends. He figured he was in good enough shape already."

I think Mary Kay gave us a longer break than she had planned, just to let Tony rest up. His normal color had returned by the time we mounted our bikes again and began the last lap of the journey to that night's hostel at the town of Espanola.

For a while I pedaled along in silence, carried along on my own thoughts. Maybe a letter would be waiting for me when we arrived. At least there would be a pay phone, and I could call Bruce. I probably didn't have enough change, though.

"You look so dreamy I bet I know what you're thinking about," said Matt, pedaling up beside me. "You're thinking about Bruce, right?"

"You don't have to be telepathic to figure that out," I said. Still it was a little unsettling the way he could read my thoughts.

"Will you have a letter yet?" he asked. "Does he write much?"

"I'm not really sure," I said, wondering again how he knew what I was thinking. "We were never separated before, except when I was in the hospital with appendicitis, and then one time when he went to Missouri for ten days to visit his cousins. But those times it was easy to take turns calling. And he came to see me in the hospital all the time."

"But you're afraid he won't be a faithful correspondent?"

"I didn't say I was afraid. I just said I wasn't sure." I doubled my efforts to climb the next rise. Why did Matt want to know so much about me and Bruce? He had hardly told me anything

64

about himself and his life back in Seattle. Maybe I shouldn't be shy about asking him questions. "Are you expecting any mail tonight?" I asked him.

"I don't know if it's been long enough. I'm trying not to build up my hopes," Matt told me.

What did he mean by that? Was he expecting a letter from someone special?

But before I could think of another leading question, Matt exclaimed, "Oh, no!" and pedaled ahead with a burst of speed. I had been so engrossed in my own thoughts that I hadn't been watching the people in front of us. But now I saw that something was wrong. Tony's bicycle lay at the side of the road. And Tony himself was sprawled at the edge of a field of alfalfa.

Matt was already kneeling beside him when I hurried up. "What happened?" I gasped. "Is he all right?"

Even before I had finished speaking, I realized what a ridiculous question it was. If Tony was all right, he wouldn't be lying on the ground, his eyes closed, his face white.

"I'm OK," he murmured through barely parted lips. It was reassuring to know that he was alive, but he still didn't move.

By now everyone was aware of the commotion. Calvin, Phyllis, and Corinna circled around us, trying to get a closer look. Elise dashed up, demanding, "What's the matter?"

Mary Kay sprang from her bike and elbowed her way through the crowd. She bent and felt Tony's wrist. "Get back, will you!" she ordered, her voice tense. "Let him breathe, for heaven's sake!"

"Looks like sunstroke," Calvin remarked. "It could be serious. And once you've had that, you can't stand much exposure to the sun again."

We all stepped back to give Tony more breathing room. What were we supposed to do in an emergency like this? If we'd been at home it would have been easy—just call a doctor. But we were out on a back road in the middle of nowhere.

I watched Mary Kay closely, hoping she'd tell us what was wrong and how to make everything right again. But even she looked scared and uncertain. "Someone better go for help," she said, but she didn't tell us who should go or where the help could be found.

It was Matt who uncapped his canteen, soaked a clean shirt from his saddlebag, and pressed it to Tony's forehead. He wedged one of his saddlebags under Tony's feet, raising them several inches from the ground.

Elise bent closer. "Tony, it's me!" she cried. "Can't you say something?"

"Relax, will you?" he said, and now his voice was gaining strength. "I'm not dead yet."

Relief washed over Mary Kay's face. "You feel better?" she asked. "Did you faint?"

Tony sat up slowly. The wet shirt fell to his lap. "Like I say, I'll live."

He eyed the canteen in Matt's hand. Matt passed it to him, and he took a long swallow before he went on. "I don't know what hit me. I started feeling kind of dizzy, but I didn't want to stop. And then the next thing I knew . . ." He shook his head as if to clear it. "The next thing I knew I was flat on the ground like a jerk."

"Listen, don't feel so bad." Mary Kay patted his shoulder. "It could happen to anybody. You'd better just take it easy for a little while."

"Maybe I can thumb a ride for him to the hostel," Matt suggested. "He probably shouldn't bike any more today."

"I don't know what headquarters would say about hitchhiking," Mary Kay said doubtfully. "But really, under the circumstances, I think it's the best idea."

Not many cars traveled along those back roads. But Matt stood on the roadside, patiently holding out his thumb. A car glided past, perhaps frightened off by the sight of so many of us. A few minutes later a red Buick slowed, then picked up speed again. As it vanished around the next curve, I read the sticker on its bumper: "I Brake For Dinosaurs."

"Guess we just weren't big enough for him," Matt said. The road stretched long and empty. There was no sound but the chirping of grasshoppers in the field. We waited.

"Really, I don't need a ride," Tony said. "I can go on my bike the rest of the way."

Matt ignored him. A battered truck lumbered toward us, and he waved frantically, stepping farther into the road. The truck slowed to a stop.

The driver cranked down his window and leaned out. "What can I do for you?" he asked with a heavy Spanish accent.

Mary Kay hurried forward. "We're on a long-distance bicycle trip," she explained. "One of the fellows in our group isn't feeling too well. Do you think you can give him a ride to the youth hostel where we're staying tonight, outside Espanola?"

The driver shook his head, and for a moment I thought he was refusing to help. "I am sorry," he said, "I not understand so good the English."

A small dark woman, who had to be his wife, nodded and smiled at us from the seat beside him. But she didn't seem to understand our problem, either. "This boy," Mary Kay began again, pointing at Tony, "is sick. We need a ride."

Phyllis approached the truck, her gaze fastened on the driver's face. *"Tiene que ir a Espanola,"* she said in her low, rough voice. *"Le pueden llevar?"*

A grin spread over the driver's face. He broke into a string of rapid-fire Spanish. Phyllis watched and nodded. Her answer was brief, but he seemed satisfied. *"Sí, sí,"* he said, opening his door and springing to the ground. He scampered behind the truck and went to lower the tailgate. "I take you, the two of you," he said, pointing to Tony and Mary Kay. "In here. Bicycles, too."

By then I had grown more aware of a chorus of shrill peeping, which swelled louder when the tailgate was down. The truck was loaded with chickens, their cages stacked one upon another in two long rows.

"I got seventy-two of them," the driver said. "Is little bit noisy, yes?"

Somehow I didn't think the noise would be the problem. But I wasn't sure how Tony and Mary Kay would endure the smell that wafted over to us like a thick cloud. It might be enough to make Tony pass out all over again.

"You don't have seventy-two chickens, you've got seventy-three," Tony muttered, getting to his feet. He stood still for a moment as though he wanted to test his legs. Though they held firm, there wasn't a trace of his old swagger as he walked to the truck and climbed aboard.

I looked over at Phyllis again as Mary Kay helped the driver load the bicycles. It had never occurred to me that she might be able to speak and lip-read Spanish as well as English. Of course, her last name was Sanchez, so I guess it only made sense. After all these days of traveling together, I was still discovering things about the other members of the group.

"I think I'd better appoint someone temporary leader," Mary Kay said. "Matt, you've been on trips before. You want to take over for a bit?"

"Sure," said Matt. "Just give me a quick refresher on the route. About four more miles down this road."

"Then it's a left turn. You go about another mile, and you'll see a sign for the hostel." She climbed into the truck beside Tony, settling in the aisle between the cages.

It was then, as I waved my goodbye, that I noticed the truck had Colorado license plates. I wondered if the driver was heading for Boulder. If I hitched a ride with him I might be at our final destination in only a few hours, instead of spending the next three weeks on the trip. But for the first time, I wasn't so keen on the idea of finishing our journey in a hurry.

I watched Matt wheel his bicycle to the head of our line. He didn't make a big issue of being placed in command, but I could tell that he was a natural leader. He looked easy and confident at the front of our little caravan, as though he'd found the place where he really belonged.

"Mrs. Dowland, the housemother here, has a nursing degree," Mary Kay explained when we arrived at the hostel. "She says Tony doesn't have sunstroke or anything serious like that. He's just a little out of shape, and it caught up with him."

"It sure looked like heatstroke to me," Calvin insisted. "That or heat prostration. Only if it were heat prostration he'd—"

"OK, Dr. Quincy, I'm not ready for the post mortem yet," Tony broke in. He lay on the sofa, sipping a tall glass of Mrs. Dowland's lemonade. He looked almost like his old self again, with even a hint of his tough-guy wink.

The hostel was quite different from the Spanish villa where we had spent our first night. It was a rambling old farmhouse that could have used a fresh coat of paint.

"Three of you have letters," announced Mrs. Dowland, appearing in the doorway of the lounge. She held them out one by one. "Matthew Jordon, Corinna Brown, Rhonda McFarland."

"How come I never get anything?" Elise grumbled. Tony said something to console her, but I wasn't really listening. I turned the envelope over and read the address in that familiar sprawling handwriting. Here it was at last, a letter from Bruce!

I sought the privacy of the wide wooden porch, settled into a wicker rocking chair, and began to read:

Dear Rhonda,

Hi! How are you doing? I'm just looking over that itinerary you left me, and I figure by the time you read this, you'll have done some pretty heavy-duty bicycling. I bet your muscles are really aching!

Things around here are the same. Dad's going to have me start taking inventory. Tonight, Monday, I went over to Jack's to shoot pool down in his basement. But Sally was there, and I felt kind of left out, so I didn't stay too long.

Well, a month isn't really such a big deal, like I say, and part of it's already passed now. I hope you're having a good time, but not too good a time, if you know what I mean, ha-ha. When you get back,

*we won't have to go through this anymore,
and everything will be back to normal.
    Bye for now.*

                                    Love,

                                    Bruce

Beneath his name ran a jaunty row of *X*'s.

I scanned the letter again, searching for something, though I wasn't quite sure what it was. Bruce didn't express himself very well in letters, neither did he over the telephone. Nowhere had he even said he missed me, exactly. But he did, I could tell by the way he said he felt out of place around Jack and Sally. And he wanted me to come home so everything could get back to normal.

I hardly deserved a boy like Bruce. How could I let myself admire Matt, even for a minute? In a few short weeks Matt would be gone from my life forever. But Bruce had known me since I was thirteen, and I knew I could always count on him.

I hunted through my pockets and found four crumpled dollar bills, but they wouldn't do me much good. "Has anybody got any spare change?" I asked, returning to the lounge. "Quarters, dimes, nickels—anything?"

Elise was nowhere in sight, probably off taking a long shower. Matt was still busy reading his letter. Tony fished a couple of quarters from his wallet, and following his lead, Phyllis dug through the pockets of her jeans and handed me three dimes and a couple of nickels.

Matt folded his letter carefully and slid it back into its envelope. "Making another long distance call?" he said, teasing me. The envelope was hidden in his hand. I could only make out the word *Seattle*. It was from his parents, maybe. Or a friend. Or someone else.

But I wasn't going to think about things like that. "Thanks," I said as he offered me two more dimes. "I've got to write down how much I owe everybody, so I can keep it all straight."

I counted the change I had collected—enough for at least five minutes, I figured. As soon as I heard his voice again I'd know for sure that nothing had changed between Bruce and me.

Clutching the coins in my fist, I hurried out to the phone and dialed his number.

Chapter Seven

We camped Saturday and Sunday nights in Rio Grande Gorge State Park, close enough to a small pond that we could plan on some swimming. I had been hauling the pots and pans all day Saturday, and I felt as if I had been carrying a load of bricks up Mount Everest. No one had been exaggerating when they talked about the extra weight. I sagged against a mossy boulder, too exhausted to move and grateful that the next day would be free for rest and relaxation. I'd swim in that quiet little pond I'd seen nearby and work on my drawings. I wouldn't even look at my bicycle all day.

"I've been thinking," Mary Kay said, setting down a bag of provisions. "It'd be a good idea to switch tent mates once in a while. It'll give you all a chance to get to know each other better."

Elise, who had been unpacking our pup tent from the rattrap, sprang up in dismay. "But Rhonda and I are used to each other," she protested. "What's the point of changing things around after all this time?"

I didn't have the energy to argue with Mary Kay, and with weary defeat I heard her answer, "I once had a teacher who said you should try something new every day. Otherwise you never learn who you really are."

She looked over the forlorn, dusty group assembled in front of her, making up her mind. "Calvin, you've had a tent to yourself long enough. You can tent with Tony tonight. And Elise with Phyllis. Rhonda and Corinna."

Elise didn't quite suppress a groan. "But isn't it better for Phyllis and Corinna to be together?" she asked, as if she had only their interests in mind. "That way they can talk to each other."

"Sure, and that way they stay isolated," Mary Kay said coolly. She turned to Phyllis and Corinna and explained the new arrangements to them, speaking slowly and carefully and gesturing to illustrate what she said. I could tell they understood because their faces, too, clouded with disappointment.

I was grateful in a way. I had been getting tired of Elise's whining complaints night after night. She could never get comfortable sleeping on the ground, she was always too hot or too cold, the mosquitoes were constantly driving her crazy. But the thought of trying to communicate with Corinna was overwhelming. This would be another of those wonderful challenges, I told myself. Mom would certainly approve.

Working together to pitch our tent was easy enough. We were both so experienced in setting up camp by now that words were unnecessary, anyway. We stowed our sleeping bags inside and rejoined the rest of the group.

Elise pouted all through supper—a green salad, barbecued chicken, and baked potatoes heated in foil. But she brightened up as soon as Matt brought out his guitar and played a funny little song about a junk-food junkie. She sat right next to him, beaming at him as if she'd never heard anyone sing before.

We were all pretty tired, and no one seemed to want to stay up very late. By ten o'clock Phyllis lay stretched on a blanket, her head pillowed on one arm, and Calvin sat yawning over the book he was trying to read by flashlight. Matt stopped singing and just let his fingers strum drowsy chords on the strings. Not even Elise was listening by that time. When he finally slipped the guitar back into its case, it was the signal for us all to stumble off toward our pup tents.

I had crawled into my sleeping bag and was just sliding into a doze when the beam of Corinna's flashlight pierced the darkness around me. Still fully dressed, she sat on her bedroll, scribbling furiously.

At first when she thrust the slip of paper at me, I tried to close my eyes and turn away. But my curiosity won out. I propped myself up on one elbow and read: "Rhonda, let's go swimming."

"Now?" I demanded.

Corinna gave a vigorous nod. She took her note back and added, "The water's warmer at night."

"You're nuts!" I exclaimed. I flipped the note over and poured out my objections: "Too tired. Too late. Too cold. Too far. Somebody might see us."

Corinna only shrugged. She dug through her saddlebag, pulled out a bathing suit, and put it on. Then she threw on shorts and a T-shirt, grabbed a yellow beach towel, and scrambled out past the tent flap.

That was my chance to go back to sleep. But instead I found myself rummaging for my flashlight. I dug a towel and my bathing suit from the bottom of my saddlebag, quickly changed, then followed Corinna out into the night.

It wasn't only that I was worried about Corinna swimming by herself—I also thought it might be fun to join her. But I still had my doubts.

Corinna was kneeling at the flap of Phyllis and Elise's tent, right next to ours. Phyllis peered out, her hair tousled, her eyes heavy with sleep. Their hands darted in the beam of Corinna's flashlight. Phyllis frowned and shook her head. But Corinna's signs flew faster, her eyes sparkling with mischief. I didn't have to know sign language to feel her powers of persuasion. Slowly Phyllis's frown melted. She was beginning to weaken.

"What's going on?" came Elise's muffled voice from inside.

"These two nuts want to go swimming!" I whispered. "You want to come?"

"Swimming!" She wriggled out of her sleeping bag. "Sure, I'm coming. Give me a second to change."

Already I had forgotten my list of objections. After all, if even Elise could leap so fearlessly into the adventure, why had I been holding back?

Soon the four of us stood outside our tents, towels slung over our arms, trying to stifle our giggles. "Watch out," Phyllis said in her deep, hoarse voice, pointing to Mary Kay's tent a few yards away. "She'll wake up."

"Keep quiet and she won't," I hissed, putting a finger to my lips. Shading our flashlights we crept past Mary Kay's silent tent. I remembered one of the NAHT pamphlets said the trip leader could send home any member who didn't abide by the rules. I'd never read a rule against swimming, but there was bound to be one about sneaking around past curfew. But the thought filled me with a delicious sense of excitement.

Once we had passed Mary Kay's tent we still weren't safe. To reach the path that led down to the pond, we had to pass the boys' tents, too. We didn't want them to wake up and alert Mary Kay. Corinna took the lead, skirting a wide arc around the first tent. But her course brought us within ten feet of the second one, which was perched on a little knoll.

Suddenly Elise gave a cry of fright. I grabbed her arm to silence her, but she jerked away, brushing frantically at her face.

"What's the matter?" I whispered. "Come on, we've got to get out of here."

"It was a bat!" Elise gasped. "I felt its wings! It zoomed right by."

An icy sensation slithered down my back, but somehow I managed to remain in control. "It wasn't a bat," I told her. "I bet it was just a big moth or something."

"You sound like Calvin," she muttered. "Anyway, moths are bad enough." Still she didn't dash back to the security of her tent. She hurried along with the rest of us.

I kept glancing back at the tent on the knoll. It was where Matt slept. Had he heard the commotion as we scurried by? Would he guess what we were up to?

The path sloped steeply down to the pond. Once Phyllis's foot dislodged a rock that started a tiny avalanche that tumbled down ahead of us. Twisted roots lurched up to trip me, and I scratched my leg on a prickly bush. But at last we stood on the stony shore of the pond, the water smooth and inviting before us.

Again it was Corinna who led our little brigade. She took off her shorts and shirt, then disappeared into the shadows down on the shore and emerged moments later sleek and glistening in the pond. Giggling and waving at us merrily, she splashed in the water.

Phyllis and Elise hesitated another few seconds. Then they, too, were in the water.

I threw my shorts, shirt, and towel next to the others and straightened up. The pebbles on the shore stung my feet, but the fresh night breeze was delicious against my unprotected skin.

"The bottom's yucky!" Elise exclaimed. "But the water's great."

The water caressed my feet and ankles, then my knees as I waded in. The bottom sloped sharply, and I let myself fall forward, yielding to the water's embrace. I rolled onto my back and drifted, barely twitching my hands and feet to stay afloat. This was total freedom. The warm water let me bend and turn and glide any way I chose.

Suddenly something seized my foot. I kicked away with a shriek of horror, imagining water snakes and swimming rats and a host of other slimy, crawly creatures.

But, of course, it was only Corinna. She surfaced beside me, giggling, and I flung a handful of water into her face. She ducked and swam away a few strokes. In the moonlight she pointed and beckoned until I understood.

Phyllis, who was a strong swimmer, was already well out into the middle of the pond. But Corinna's scheme was to sneak up on Elise, who floated dreamily on her back, lost to the world. We separated so that one of us could approach her from either side and swam toward her under water. At almost the same instant, we each grabbed one of her trailing feet.

Elise let out a scream of fright, kicking and thrashing and spluttering. "You rats!" she cried when we surfaced, laughing, and let her go. "What are you trying to do? I thought it was a shark or something."

"OK! We know you're out there!" a boy's voice shouted.

All three of us plunged instantly beneath the surface. It had been Tony's voice, there could be no mistake. If only I could have stayed down there, burrowed among the rocks and roots at the bottom of the pond. But already my lungs were demanding air, I couldn't hold out much longer.

My head broke the surface, and I began to tread water. Elise, Phyllis, and Corinna had also come up for air. "We see you!" Matt shouted. "You can't hide from us!" Three flashlight beams swept across the water, seeking us out.

"I told you they were down here!" It was Calvin's voice.

My instincts had been right in the beginning. I never should have let Corinna convince me to come out.

Phyllis and Corinna started to paddle to the shore, and I swam after them. That glorious sense of freedom had disappeared completely. The water was cold now, and tendrils of weeds wrapped themselves around my ankles. I longed to get out of the pond and be warm and asleep in my tent again.

"What's going on down here?"

A new, broader flashlight beam played over the boys on the bank. A figure emerged from the woods. "I thought I heard something or someone going by my tent," Mary Kay said. "What's happening?"

"We didn't do anything," Calvin said. "We just came down for a midnight swim."

Tony guffawed. "Yeah, only the girls were in the water ahead of us."

Mary Kay threw the beam of her flashlight out over the pond. What was she going to do? Maybe this would bring the whole trip to a halt. I'd be sent home in disgrace.

"All right," Mary Kay said at last. "All the guys are going back to camp. You ladies have exactly two minutes to get dried off and dressed."

A groan rose from the shore, but the boys turned back to the woods, their lights bobbing up the path. Mary Kay waited as we swam to shore and collected our towels.

"Look, as far as I'm concerned, you didn't do anything all that bad," Mary Kay said awkwardly as I pulled my T-shirt over my head. "It's just that, in my position, you know, I've got to think about the rules."

I held my breath. Now she was going to say it. The trip was off. We would all be sent back home. But it wasn't fair! The summer was only beginning! Who would have guessed that switching tent mates would lead to all this?

"But this really isn't any big deal," Mary Kay went on. "Let's just forget it. No point getting them all stirred up back at headquarters." She hesitated and added, "The first time I went on an NAHT trip a bunch of us did the same thing."

"You did!" I exclaimed. "Really?"

"So we won't tell anybody about tonight," she concluded, "as long as nothing like this ever happens again."

A tide of relief washed over me, and I wondered why I had ever longed to get the summer over with quickly and return home.

"Why does she have to act like such a big shot?" Elise muttered. "I swear, some people!"

"She could have been a whole lot worse," I pointed out. We were all quiet after that, climbing single file up the path to our tents and what remained of our good night's sleep.

Chapter Eight

On Monday afternoon when we reached the next youth hostel outside the little town of Tres Piedras, nearly a dozen bicycles already stood in the racks out back. "This will be fun," Matt told me. "We're going to meet another trip."

I was hot and sweaty after thirty-eight miles on the road. All I wanted was a long, uninterrupted shower and a bed with clean, crisp sheets. But when we crossed the wooden porch and entered the kitchen, we found a bustle of activity. Three girls were singing a round as two of them chopped vegetables and the third stirred something in a big pot on the stove. A shaggy-haired boy in patched jeans sat mending the seam of a canvas saddlebag. Voices drifted in from other rooms, calling to one another, bright with excitement.

For three days, since we left the hostel at Espanola, our group had traveled alone, passing through the world but somehow isolated from it. Now suddenly we were surrounded by outsiders. As Matt said, it would be fun to meet them, to break up the routine. But at the same time I found myself wishing we had found the hostel empty. The eight of us had developed our own ways of being together and our own private jokes now, and I wasn't sure I wanted to share this with anyone new.

"Where are you people headed?" Matt asked, swinging onto a stool by the long, Formica-topped counter.

"We're on a cross-country marathon," said the shaggy-haired boy, folding the scissors back into his Swiss army knife. "We left San Francisco back on June thirteenth."

"We were doing seventy miles a day, until we hit these mountains," put in the girl at the stove. "Sometimes I feel like I'm pedaling in my sleep."

I had felt so exhausted those first few days of the trip. But now the long miles day after day didn't seem to bother me as much. It had become easier to meet the challenge.

But apparently Elise didn't feel the same way. "Seventy miles a day! What we're doing is bad enough," she said. "I still don't know if I'm going to make it. My blisters have got blisters."

"Come on, you're doing fine." Matt threw her a warm, reassuring smile. "Don't put yourself down all the time."

Lately it seemed he was always giving Elise extra attention, telling her she could make it up the next hill, helping her lash her saddlebags and rattrap to the fender of her bike, pumping air into her front tire. He almost never did things like that for me. But what business was that of mine? I asked myself.

We wouldn't be able to start our own cooking until the marathoners finished their supper. I wandered out to the living room and introduced myself to two more members of the new group, Lucy and Joanna. They were busy giggling over something that had happened on the road that morning—someone named David had gone racing ahead, taken a wrong turn, and spent the rest of the day trying to catch up with the others. They made no effort to include me in their conversation. Finally I got restless and went to study the bookshelf beside the wide brick fireplace.

The books were an odd collection—a travelogue about points of interest in New Mexico, a set of field guides to southwestern birds, trees, and flowers, a few volumes of the 1978 *Encyclopaedia Britannica*, and a random assortment of novels.

Of course I had to call Bruce after supper. He'd be expecting to hear from me. But I really didn't have much to say to him, only that I was tired. I couldn't tell him about Matt and Elise. After all, what right did I have to care what went on between them? Since I didn't want to talk to Bruce right then, I went back to the living room and wrote a letter to my parents.

At supper Elise seated herself next to Matt at the long wooden table, whispering and giggling to him all through the meal. Afterward, while Calvin and I washed pots and pans in the big double sink, they loaded plates and silverware into the restaurant-style dishwasher. I couldn't catch their words over the clatter and the rush of running water, but every now and then Elise gave a high trill of laughter.

It was a relief to escape to the pay phone. Bruce's father answered my call. The precious seconds I had bought ticked steadily away while he summoned Bruce from the basement. "Oh, hi," he said when he heard my voice. "I figured it'd be you."

Something was strange about his tone of voice. "What were you doing?" I asked. "I interrupted something?"

"Not really. It's just that a couple of people are over here. You remember that old Ping-Pong table of Dad's? We finally set up, and we were downstairs playing doubles."

"Who's down there?" I asked.

"Oh, Jack and Sally and"—he hesitated—"and this girlfriend of Sally's, somebody she met at the swim club she belongs to."

"Oh." The word dropped heavy as a stone between us. But after all, she was just a friend of Jack's girlfriend. And they were only playing a little Ping-Pong together. "What's her name?" I asked, trying to sound unconcerned. "Is she nice?"

There was something a little uneven about the way Bruce answered. "She's just a girl. Her name's Melissa Snow." Before I could comment he plunged on, "So how's the trip going? You're still all in one piece and everything?"

"Yeah, I'm fine. I sent you a letter yesterday, with sketches of some of the people in my group. Maybe you'll get it tomorrow."

"Please deposit sixty cents for the next three minutes or your call will be terminated," broke in a metallic female voice.

I was counting out more dimes and quarters

from the stack on the table beside me when Bruce said, "Listen, maybe we may as well say goodbye for now, anyway. This is costing you."

He had never worried about the cost of our calls before. But Bruce and I really didn't have much to say right then. "Well, OK," I told him. "I'll call you next time I get near a phone."

"Yeah, you do that," Bruce said with a flash of his old warmth. "I'll be waiting for you."

"Goodbye!" I called. "Talk to you soon."

The sounds of a guitar and girls singing loudly drifted out from the living room. I went to see what was going on, all the while picturing Bruce returning to his game with Jack, Sally, and Melissa Snow.

Matt sat on a straight chair in the living room, strumming his guitar. In a semicircle on the rug sat Lucy, Joanna, and the girls who had been singing in the kitchen. Elise sat on a stool close by his side, gazing up at him in rapture. Tony was nowhere in sight. If he liked Elise as much as I had begun to suspect he did, he probably couldn't stand to watch her right now.

"I want to try out a new song tonight, while I've got so many critics around," Matt said after his last verse came to its rollicking close. "I've been working on it for the past few days."

As I slipped into the group gathered around him, he added in a low voice, "It's for somebody special, somebody I've been thinking about a lot lately."

A hint of the melody was woven into his opening chords. Then Matt began to sing. His rich, full voice was so soft that I had to lean forward to catch all of the words:

"Your comings and your goings and your
    little turns of mind,
I see them every day and never wonder.
There are times I just don't see you,
    till those moments when I find
That the thought of you can shake my
    soul like thunder."

I wondered who the special person was who Matt had been thinking about so much these past few days. A pink flush tinged Elise's cheeks, and she swayed very gently to the music as though Matt had written the song just for her.

A knot drew tight in the pit of my stomach. Matt and I had started the trip as friends. And he was still friendly to me, I couldn't deny that. I shouldn't be watching Matt and Elise at all. I ought to be worrying why Bruce had sounded so strange earlier on the phone and why he was spending time with Melissa Snow.

"So I think I'm gonna tell you just how

much I really care,
That I'll be with you when the road gets
steep and narrow,
Yes, I really want to tell you there's
a lot that we can share,
And I think I'm gonna say it all
tomorrow."

He sang the last stanza again, and Elise joined him on the final line: "I think I'm gonna say it all, tomorrow."

All the girls around me burst into delighted "oohs" and "aahs." Matt beamed with pleasure, but he asked, "Doesn't anybody have any suggestions? Now's your chance."

Everyone insisted that the song was perfect just as it was. "I wouldn't change a note or a word of it, not for the world," Elise cooed. That was about as much as I could stand. I rose quietly and stole out to the back porch with *Little Dorrit*, a book I had chosen from the living room shelves.

But even outside I couldn't find any peace. Laughter bubbled out through the open windows. Now Matt was singing a silly song about the cockroach that ate Cincinnati, and soon the others were joining in on the choruses.

I had only reached page six of the book when the shaggy-haired boy from the marathon group emerged from the hostel and sat on the porch railing. He unclipped his Swiss army knife from his belt and began whittling at a piece of wood.

His presence made it harder than ever to get caught up in the novel. "What are you making?" I asked.

He frowned at the litter of chips and shavings that was collecting around his feet. "I don't know. A mess, it looks like."

He held up the piece of wood for my inspection. A large chunk had been removed from the top, and a ragged groove ran along one side.

"I'm not sure exactly what I'm doing," he explained. "I just thought it'd be neat to try and learn to carve, you know, like the old-timers do in the movies."

"Have you got a book on it or something?"

He shook his head, and a lock of hair tumbled into his eyes. "No," he said, brushing it back. "I just thought I'd figure it out on my own. This was going to be a sailboat."

"A sailboat?" I repeated. He certainly did have a long way to go.

"Well, now I'm thinking it'll end up as a barge." He gave a little laugh, then put the wood aside and studied the book in my hand. "Do you *like* reading that?" he asked. "It looks deadly."

"So far it is," I said, snapping it shut and giving him my full attention. "I guess I'm just not in the mood."

"I don't think I told you my name," he said. "I'm David Marcus."

"Hi, I'm Rhonda McFarland." Something clicked in my memory. "Are you the David who got lost today?"

"Boy, word sure gets around, doesn't it?" he said sheepishly. "But I was just thinking, do you feel like going for a walk? We could climb that hill over there and maybe look at the stars."

"Oh, do you know about the stars?" I asked eagerly.

But again David shook his head. "About all I can recognize is the Big Dipper," he said. "But it'd be fun to climb up there and look, wouldn't it?"

"Sure." There was something appealing about the way he confessed that he didn't know what he was doing.

As we started down the back steps, I noticed that the singing and strumming of the guitar had stopped. What were Matt and Elise doing now? Had they found some private little nook where he could sing his songs to her undisturbed? Well, let them, I told myself. If Matt didn't care to spend his time with me, I could always find someone else.

We had crossed the yard when a shout from

behind us made me stop short. "Hey, Rhonda! Where are you going?"

Something in my chest fluttered uncontrollably as I spun around.

"We're going to make s'mores," Matt said, hurrying toward us. "I was looking all over for you."

"You were?" Hastily I tried to hide the excitement I felt. "What are s'mores?"

"You never had them? You toast a marshmallow, and then you put it between two squares from a Hershey chocolate bar, and you make it into a sandwich with graham crackers," Matt said.

"And it's so good you're supposed to ask for some more," David added. "I forgot that the people from our group bought that stuff this afternoon." He looked at me questioningly. "You still want to go for that walk, or would you rather go back in?"

David was really nice, someone I would enjoy getting to know. But the way I was starting to feel about Matt was different. And Matt had left Elise and the others to come all the way out there, just looking for me.

I hesitated just long enough to be polite. "Well, the mosquitoes out here are getting pretty bad," I said. "And I've never had a s'more."

David's disappointment showed only for an instant before he laughed it away. "Try one and have some more and some more," he said and trailed after me and Matt back across the yard to the hostel.

Chapter Nine

Matt rode beside me all the next afternoon. The going was pretty steep most of the way, so we didn't talk much. But somehow it gave me a warm feeling whenever I glanced over at his tall, lanky figure, and now and then a smile flashed my way that had his green eyes sparkling. Maybe Elise had never meant anything to him. Whenever we exchanged a look or a word, I felt something special was springing up between Matt and me.

Toward five o'clock we came over a crest and saw that Mary Kay ahd dismounted from her bicycle and was waving our whole procession to a halt.

"This is the place, in case you want to make it a ceremonial occasion," she said. "The Colorado line is right up ahead."

"This is a moment we shall all remember," Matt proclaimed. "At four forty-seven, on this date, Tuesday, July second, our fearless leader will lead us across the line into a brand-new state."

"Into a brand-new state of confusion," concluded Calvin, and laughing we pedaled down the slope and passed the sign that announced "Welcome to Colorado."

"I guess it's me," I said slowly. "I don't feel like the same person I was back there."

Why had I ever fought so hard to stay at home in Kankakee? Already I was clinging to each passing day of the trip, dreading the time when it would all be over and I would sink back into my old routine. I wished I could tell Matt about last night's conversation with Bruce, about my uneasy feeling that we had less and less to say to each other in our letters and phone calls. I was beginning to wonder if we had ever had much to talk about besides school gossip and which movie we'd like to see. What I always thought was a real caring for each other now seemed like little more than habit.

But I didn't try to put any of these tangled thoughts into words. We were approaching another rise, and we put our effort back into pedaling, cutting our way deeper into the State of Colorado with every turn of the wheels.

That night Elise and I headed out of our new camp to gather firewood. "It's too bad there aren't more boys in our group," Elise said. "But Matt makes it interesting enough."

Matt had been playing his new song, which just ended, "I think I'm gonna say it all tomorrow." I wondered if he'd had a private talk with Elise that day. "What about Tony?" I asked hopefully. "I think he kind of likes you."

Elise shrugged. "He's OK," she said, "but you've got to admit Matt's much cuter. And he's just more self-assured, you know?"

I knew, all right. Matt was good-looking, with his lean, muscular body, his reddish blond curls, and a face that was always alert to everything. But there was more to him than his looks, something in his sturdy self-assurance that made him hard to resist.

Now, talking about him to Elise, my confidence was shaken. Elise was so daintily feminine. With my straight blond hair that was always tangling in the wind, my plain, angular face, and my big calloused hands, I always felt a little awkward and unkempt beside her. What could Matt ever see in a girl like me?

I'd been going with Bruce for so long that I hardly ever thought about how other boys thought of me. I'd always considered that was one of the advantages of having a steady boyfriend—not having to compete endlessly with other girls who were much prettier than I was and who knew just the right things to say in any situation. I thought of myself as plain and quiet, but Bruce liked me just the way I was.

Slowly Elise and I worked our way back to camp, both of us carrying hefty bundles of kindling. As soon as we arrived, I began searching for Matt.

He was whistling softly as he and Calvin sliced onions on a flat stump, so intent on his chore that he barely glanced up when we dumped our wood by the fireplace.

Phyllis helped me get the fire started, but Elise surprised me by volunteering to begin the cooking.

"I could help you," I protested. "And Corinna and Tony aren't doing anything—look at them lounging around over there."

"No, you go relax," Elise insisted. "I've got everything under control."

She looked like she meant what she said. I got out my sketch pad and sat in a hollow between two big rocks to touch up a few of my earlier drawings. The countryside was becoming more exciting day by day. The rolling hills were gradually giving way to jagged mountain peaks. The bicycling was harder now, though Mary Kay still found routes around the toughest places. But sometimes I was so caught up in the view, I didn't even notice the weary aching in my legs.

It was impossible to capture the landscape on paper, no matter how doggedly I tried. The picture I had started earlier on our lunch break, a mountain peak lost in clouds, looked like a child's drawing to me now.

Sighing, I put it aside. Something drew my gaze back to Matt, and now I understood all too well why Elise had wanted to cook supper herself. While I had been busy with my pencils, Matt had gone over to offer his assistance. She might tell *me* she had things under control, but when Matt was around, she became utterly helpless.

Her high trill of laughter floated to me on the wind. "Matt! What else should I put into the stew?"

It annoyed me, the way she threw herself at him. But if that was what he wanted in a girl, then he deserved her. I turned away from them and tried to go back to my drawings again. I skipped the one I had drawn the previous day of cows and a horse grazing in a fenced field, and came to the set of portraits I was attempting of members of the group. There was Calvin, frowning over a book. But my pencils couldn't show the way his pasty complexion was turning healthy and tan. And I couldn't capture Tony's brash swagger, the way he put his shoulders back and thrust his chin foward as if he were ready to attack the whole world. And how could I hope to do justice to Matt? Perhaps I should give up drawing and learn to knit sweaters instead, I thought. At least I'd be doing something practical.

"The stew will be done in a little while now." My head jerked up at the sound of Matt's voice right behind me, and hastily I flipped the page over.

"Don't let me interrupt you," he said, but he leaned forward, trying to see what I was working on. "I was just thinking if you run out of things to do, maybe you'd like to borrow this book of mine."

He held out a thick paperback, and I read the title aloud. "*The Milagro Beanfield War.* What's it about?"

"It all takes place in New Mexico, in the country we just went through," Matt said. "It's about Mexican-American farmers fighting for their rights to the water and the land. This friend of mine gave it to me before I left on the trip, and it gave me a real feel for this part of the country."

"What made you decide to lend it to me?"

Matt shrugged. "I saw you reading *Little Dorrit* at Tres Piedras last night," he said. "I figured you must be desperate. This book will really move you."

Matt had seemed so busy with Elise and his circle of admirers at the hostel at Tres Piedras, yet even when I felt I was invisible to him, he had still noticed me.

"It's not my fault!" Tony's voice rose above the clatter of pots and pans. "I left everything in one pile when I washed the dishes at lunchtime."

Matt and I crossed the clearing to the camp fire. "You sure you didn't just leave it lying there by the side of the road?" Calvin demanded. "The other day you would've forgotten your saddlebag if I hadn't—"

"Yeah, well, that was then. I sure didn't lose the potato peeler," Tony said, scowling.

Mary Kay tried to make peace. "Let's all look carefully through our things," she suggested. "It'll turn up somewhere."

I unfastened my rattrap and rummaged through its contents, though I knew I certainly didn't have the potato peeler with me. I was opening my first saddlebag when a cry of triumph from Tony made me spring to my feet.

"You've got it right there! Look at that! Why'd you try to pin everything on me?"

I couldn't help laughing at the sheepish

expression on Calvin's face as he held up the potato peeler. "I don't remember putting it in my saddlebag," he said, shaking his head. But he rallied quickly. "The phantom put it there, to incriminate me. You know, Clarke Dawson."

We all giggled. Clarke Dawson had never contacted Mary Kay at any of the hostels. But in his absence he had become our company mascot.

At last, when supper was over and the dishes were scrubbed, I retreated to my hollow with *The Milagro Beanfield War.* Matt would want to know what I thought of it, so I'd have to read very carefully and think of some intelligent comments to make. As I opened the book I felt a little like I was diving into a school assignment, even though it was an assignment I wouldn't have turned down for the world.

Matt was right. The story did sweep right along. Before I realized how much time had sped by, I was almost finished with Part One, reading by the dying light of the sun. I'd have to get my flashlight if I wanted to read any more that evening.

I flipped back through the pages I had read to glance at the quotations from reviewers in the front. Suddenly a few handwritten lines on the first page grabbed my attention. Someone had inscribed a message: "To Matt, to let you know I'll be thinking of you this summer. Jenny."

I closed the book very slowly and sat still. Jenny. I imagined a tall, fair girl with light brown hair flowing down past her shoulders. She'd look as polished and feminine as Elise, but there would be nothing helpless about her. She'd be excellent at tennis or ice skating or maybe ballet. And she'd have the strength to be brave, even though Matt went off on hosteling trips summer after summer.

I shook my head as though I could jar her out of my thoughts. I'd promised myself I wouldn't dwell on Matt so much. He had his own life, and I had mine. It was only natural that someone was waiting for him back in Seattle. He had Jenny, just as I had Bruce.

Bruce had sounded so funny on the phone. If I'd been back home I would have wondered all day about his odd, hasty tone and his Ping-Pong match with Melissa Snow. But instead I was wondering about Jenny, who had promised to think of Matt all summer.

Maybe Bruce had sensed a change in me. I decided to write him a long, heartfelt letter that would bring us close together again. When I got back to Kankakee, everything would be all right.

I crawled into the pup tent I was sharing that night with Phyllis and dug my flashlight and a sweater out of my saddlebag. Now that the sun was down, the evening chill drove me closer to the camp fire. The others were laughing over a story Tony was telling about the way he'd gotten revenge on the meanest teacher in his school. I sat at the edge of the group and barely listened as I began to write: "Dear Bruce, It sure was good talking to you last night. How did you do at Ping-Pong? I'm glad you finally got that old table set up. I know you wanted to."

I set my pen down and read through what I'd just written. The words were rough and awkward, and none of my true feelings were expressed. It *hadn't* been good talking to him the night before, and I didn't care in the least who'd won his Ping-Pong game.

Bruce and I had never done much talking about the way we felt, and in a letter it was even harder to say what was on my mind. Probably Matt and Jenny could tell each other their deepest feelings in their letters.

"Dear Bruce," I began again. "So much is happening to me this summer that I don't know how to describe it all to you. It's not just that the country out here is so beautiful. It's that it's so different, being away from home and living so close to all these new people. I can hardly believe there was ever a time when I didn't know Elise and Corinna and Matt."

Why hadn't Matt ever told me about Jenny? He was always asking me questions about myself, but he kept his own life a big secret. It just wasn't fair!

With a flash of anger I started Bruce's letter over again: "You can't imagine what some of the people on this trip are like. They're really strange, and I'm with them day in and day out with nowhere to escape. Sometimes I don't know how I'm going to stand it till the end of the trip, but I've made it through almost the first half, so I guess I can hang in the rest of the way."

The first half? I paused to calculate, ticking off the days on my fingers. That day was Tuesday. Friday would be the halfway mark. In a little over two weeks I'd see Bruce again. In a little over two weeks I'd say goodbye to Matt forever.

And how could I say goodbye to Matt forever?

I crumpled the pages I had started and got to my feet. I couldn't write to Bruce that night. I couldn't even keep him in my thoughts—Matt kept pushing him aside.

Over by the fire Phyllis was trying to teach Calvin to play cat's cradle. For once Calvin was silent as he watched her intently and struggled to imitate the deft movements of her hands. He even laughed as the string tangled around his thumbs. "This isn't my thing," he admitted. "Why don't you let me teach you to play chess?"

Elise was busy filing her nails—she said a manicure was her last link with civilization. As usual Tony had his Walkman on and was tapping his foot to a beat no one else could hear. Matt sat with his back against a rock, picking soft, lilting chords on his guitar. I didn't know what I wanted to say to him, but my feet led me straight to his side.

He reached the end of the little melody he was playing and looked up. "Oh, hi," he said. "Did you start the book?"

"I read the first part."

"What did you think so far?" His hands brushed lightly across the strings, sending up a shower of silver notes.

"I like it," I said. But I couldn't remember any of the points for discussion I had set aside.

I wasn't any good at concealing my feelings for Matt. If I didn't want him to suspect that something was bothering me, now was my chance to get out of his sight. But before I could turn away, Matt asked, "Something the matter?"

"No," I said quickly. "I'll talk to you about it when I've finished—the book, I mean."

Maybe I still could have gotten away. But my feet wouldn't move, and suddenly a question burst out over the gentle strumming of the guitar. "Who's Jenny?"

For just an instant Matt's hands tensed, deadening the strings. But it was only for an instant. He broke into something new, something with a snappy beat that sounded vaguely Spanish, and said casually, "Oh, she's just this girl I know from back home."

"She can't be just any girl," I said, plunging ahead. "She says she'll be thinking about you all summer."

"She's the serious type," Matt said. "She thinks about all sorts of things."

I felt as if I were on my bike, speeding out of control down a steep hill. "And you think a lot about her, too?"

"Oh, I don't know. Not enough, maybe. I'd even forgotten that she wrote something in the front of that book."

I wasn't really getting anywhere. But I tried again. "What's she like? How long have you known her?"

"She's a little shorter than you are, with short, dark hair," he said. "She's going to be a senior. I've known her a couple of years now."

He struck a powerful chord and broke into a vigorous flamenco. It was such a change of pace that its message was unmistakable. The discussion of Jenny was closed.

And why had I pursued it in the first place? I sat alone in my hollow until Mary Kay called out that we had an especially long haul the next day and that it was time for all of us to turn in for the night.

Chapter Ten

"I thought this was supposed to be a hosteling trip," Elise interrupted as we coasted down a last stretch of road to the campsite. "All we ever do is pitch tents!"

For once I couldn't blame Elise for complaining. That night I was ready for the trip to be over.

I hadn't slept well the night before after my talk with Matt, so I was in a ferociously rotten mood. I was tired of pulling wrinkled and twisted clothes out of my saddlebag each morning. I was sick of going for long, sweaty days without a shower. My hair hung limp and stringy, and dirt was ground into the calluses on my palms.

The people in the group had suddenly begun to irritate me. Elise's complaints grated like the screech of chalk on a blackboard. I thought I'd scream if Corinna tried to pull one more prank. Tony was brasher than ever, always trying to prove that he was tougher than anyone else. As usual, Calvin had an answer for everything, and the worst part was that I never had the satisfaction of proving him wrong. And I couldn't look at Matt without thinking of Jenny. Why hadn't he told me about her right from the start?

I had to admit, though, that this was one of the most beautiful spots we had camped in so far. We had biked down into a long, narrow valley with glorious mountain peaks towering all around us.

"Well, let's see, whose turn to tent with whom?" Mary Kay looked us over critically as we were unpacking our gear. If only she'd assign me with Phyllis, I thought. Phyllis was about the only member of the group I could tolerate that day, and that was only because she kept to herself. I barely had to deal with her even when we shared a tiny pup tent.

But I should have known that I'd be out of luck. "Phyllis and Corinna haven't been together for a while," Mary Kay decided, sweeping them together with a gesture of her hands. "And Rhonda and Elise." In my foul mood I decided that was just like Mary Kay, always bossing people around. She wasn't so much older than we were, so why did she act like such a big shot?

Elise and I pitched our pup tent after supper—gooey macaroni and cheese, which Tony had insisted on cooking although we all warned him that it would never turn out right over an open fire. Elise was actually pretty good at putting the tent up by now. This time she didn't even plead for help, but set right to work before I could give directions.

I thought that I should finish Matt's book and give it back to him. But ever since I had read Jenny's inscription, I'd found it hard to care much about the action of the story.

As usual everyone was gathered around the crackling camp fire. The prospect of all that togetherness made *The Milagro Beanfield War* a bit more appealing. But before I could turn away Mary Kay said, "Come here, Rhonda. Don't isolate yourself all the time. We're going to tell stories."

Why shouldn't I isolate myself, I wanted to snap. How else was I supposed to keep from going crazy? But I took a seat on someone's bedroll at the edge of the circle. "What kind of stories?" I asked.

"I was thinking of this game where one person starts a story, and the next person has to continue it," Mary Kay said. "And you go around the group that way."

"Sounds like something little kids do at summer camp," Calvin said and groaned.

"You're the one who said you were so bored," Tony said, scowling. "You got any better suggestions?" I wasn't the only one with frayed nerves that night. I thought Calvin would come out with some sort of smart answer, but he just sat against the tree trunk and sulked.

"I've got a story," Elise said suddenly. A ring of expectant faces turned toward her.

She cleared her throat. "It's kind of a spooky one. See, there was this couple—my sister's best friend actually knew the boy. Anyway, one night they were on their way home from the movies, and they got a flat tire. So they were sitting there in the car waiting for somebody to come along and help them, and on the radio they heard that some guy had escaped from the state mental hospital just down the road from where they were stuck. They said this guy was very dangerous, and the way you could recognize him was he had one hand missing and wore a hook."

"Oh, I've heard this one," Calvin muttered, and Tony said, "What was the matter with that guy—he didn't know how to change a tire himself?"

When everyone was quiet again, Elise went on,

"It was really dark out, and all of a sudden they heard footsteps and this rattling noise—first at one door and then at the other one. The doors were all locked, though, and finally the footsteps went away.

"And then after a while a state trooper came along to see what was the matter. And when he got up to their car, he freaked out and he said, 'What's this?' And—"

"And there was a hook hanging on the door handle," Calvin finished for her. "That didn't happen to anyone you know. That story's as old as the hills."

"Can't you just lay off?" Matt exclaimed. "Let somebody else have the floor once in a while."

A few days earlier I would have winced, asking myself why he always leaped to Elise's defense. But now I knew that Elise didn't really matter to him any more than I did. The only one Matt cared about was Jenny in Seattle.

"What happened? What was it?" demanded Phyllis. She'd been reading the story from Elise's lips and translating it for Corinna, but she had lost the ending when Calvin broke in.

"A hook," Calvin repeated for her, and her hand shaped it for an instant in the air.

"It *did* happen," Elise insisted.

"Yeah, it probably did," Calvin said, and I felt that he was trying to make peace.

"I heard a weird story once," I said, surprising myself a little because I never liked to talk in front of a crowd. "It happened at the University of Illinois, not too far from where I live."

I waited for Calvin to snicker, but everyone seemed to be listening. Phyllis twisted around to get a better view of my face, and Corinna watched her hands expectantly. Now that I'd gone this far, I'd have to finish.

"Well, there were two girls who were roommates," I began. "And they ended up staying in the dorm over spring vacation—they both had a lot of studying to do or something. Anyway, they were practically the only people left in the whole dorm.

"So this one night one of them gets up to go to the bathroom down the hall. And while she's in there, she hears the bathroom window open and then this noise like somebody climbing in.

"Well, she's pretty scared, naturally. But she's in this stall, so she lifts up her feet so nobody can see them under the door, and she waits like that while heavy footsteps cross the bathroom floor and go out into the hall. And then she doesn't know what to do. There's nobody to run to for help, and besides, she doesn't want to meet this character in the hall, so she just sits there kind of panicking. And after a while the door opens again, and the footsteps cross the bathroom, and she hears the person climb back out the window."

"Is that all?" Elise asked. "That's not much of a story."

"No, that's not all," I said. "This is the awful part coming up. She goes running back to her room to tell her roommate what happened—and there's her roommate lying on the floor, strangled to death!"

A gasp ran around the circle of listeners. The wind rustled through the pine branches, and a low, wailing cry came drifting from the distance. Could it be a coyote? I edged myself closer to the crackling fire.

"I've got a story," said Matt. "I mean, if people are up for another one."

"Go on, go on!" Elise urged. "I'm not scared."

"Well, OK, then," Matt said, a note of warning in his voice. "A long time ago this family moved into a tumble-down old house. The people in the town told them that the house was haunted, but they said they weren't afraid of anything, and they moved in.

"Well, the first night they slept there the son woke up, and he heard this strange noise. *Rap, rap, rap! Rap, rap, rap!* He couldn't figure out where it was coming from, but he wasn't all that scared, so he went back to sleep.

"But then the next night he woke up again,

and there was the same weird noise. *Rap, rap, rap! Rap, rap, rap!* At this time it seemed a little closer. But he told himself that he wouldn't let it get to him, and he went back to sleep.

"But then, the next night, he woke again, and this time it sounded like it was right in the next room. So he got up to investigate. And he followed the sound: *Rap, rap, rap! Rap, rap, rap!*

"He followed it into the dark hallway, and he came to a closed door. And he listened there for a minute, gathering up his courage, then he flung the door wide open! And what did he see?" He paused to let our imaginations conjure up scenes of mayhem. "Wrapping paper!"

For a second or two we all just sat there, bewildered. Then Tony started to laugh, and pretty soon the rest of us were laughing, too. "Wrapping paper!" I repeated. "Oh, come on!"

"I thought we needed a change of pace," Matt said. "Otherwise we'd be hearing axe murderers in the woods all night long."

The tone of the evening did change after that. Instead of telling ghost stories, we wound up telling all the jokes we could remember. After a while Mary Kay asked Matt where his guitar was, and he got it out and sang a couple of funny songs, teaching us one called "Rickety Tickety Tin," about a fair young maid who "did not have her family long" because "she did every one of them in." And of course there was his song about the junk-food junkie that always made us laugh no matter how many times we heard it. He was into the third stanza when I realized that my irritation with the group had completely melted away. It had disappeared gradually, and now I could hardly remember what had caused it in the first place. The evening had turned out to be a lot of fun, despite my initial gloom. By the time we doused the camp fire and went off to our tents, I was sure I'd never find a more wonderful set of friends.

Elise dropped off to sleep right away, but I lay wide awake, listening to all the little rustlings of the woods. Matt hadn't singled me out that night for special attention, and when I thought of him, a strange yearning stirred deep inside me.

Just outside the tent, a twig snapped.

I sat bolt upright, the top of my head grazing the canvas top. The sound had not been the mere rustle of some tiny woodland creature. It was the crack of a dried branch beneath a firm, heavy foot.

No, I must've imagined it, I thought. All those ghost stories had made me jumpy.

But just when I convinced myself that the sound came from inside my own head, something scraped along the side of the tent.

Elise woke at my little shriek of fright. "Rhonda!" she cried. "What's the matter?"

"Shsh! Listen!" I found my flashlight and switched it on.

"Listen to what?" Now Elise was sitting up and hunting for her flashlight, too.

"Just listen, will you?"

For a long moment there was no sound but the endless chirping of crickets. Then, very distinctly, something slapped against the tent wall.

Elise screeched and buried her face in her hands. But by now reason was starting to overcome the wild twists of my imagination. "I bet it's the guys," I whispered. "They're out there trying to scare us."

Elise uncovered her face. "You think so? I bet it's Tony. He's the one who'd come up with a trick like that."

"Let's sneak out and catch them in the act," I said in a lcw voice.

Elise gasped. "But what if it *isn't* them? What if it's an escaped lunatic or something!"

That was a possibility I wasn't going to think about. "Yeah, sure," I said, trying to laugh us both into being brave. "It's a guy that wears this steel hook."

I squirmed out of my sleeping bag and pulled on my clothes. "Come on," I whispered. "Let's go see what they're up to."

I unzipped the tent flap, and we thrust our heads out into the chilly night air. Our flashlights played over the empty clearing. If the boys had been hiding by our tent, they certainly weren't around now—and I felt a little trickle of fear at the back of my neck. What if I was wrong? What if someone—someone demented and dangerous—*had* been prowling around?

"Look!" hissed Elise. "Up there!"

Above us, from a jagged outcropping of rock, shone a wavering beam of light.

"It's got to be them!" I said, wriggling out of the tent and getting to my feet. "Come on."

For a moment Elise hesitated. But at last she emerged, giggling, and stood beside me. "You want to just go straight up there?" she asked. "They'll see us coming, won't they?"

"I know what," I said. "You start climbing up there and keep them distracted. In the meantime I'll sneak around behind them and scare them. We'll get back at them for trying to scare us."

Elise objected, just as I'd figured she would. "You want me to walk across the clearing and climb up there all by myself? What if it's not them?"

I didn't give her a chance to argue. "It's them, I know it is. Start climbing. Pretend you don't want them to see you, but make sure they do."

Switching off my flashlight, I slipped into the shadows behind a huge boulder. I could see well enough by the light of the half-moon. I detoured around a heap of tangled brush and began to climb up the rock face through a narrow gorge. Somehow, even in the semidarkness, I managed to find toeholds.

At last I reached a plateau. I paused to catch my breath and to get my bearings. Below me bobbed Elise's light, shining out for attention. The boys couldn't be far off now. I even thought I heard Tony's teasing laugh and a muffled exclamation from Calvin. I crept along my ledge, drawn toward the sounds, searching the crevices above me for a sign of movement.

I never heard a sound behind me. But suddenly, out of nowhere, a pair of arms seized me.

"No use trying to get away! I've got you now!"

"Matt!" I knew his voice even before I recognized the familiar tall, slim figure, the green eyes laughing down at me.

"Who'd you think I was?" he asked. "Were you really scared?"

"Well, of course I was! What did you expect, coming at me like that! You want to give me a heart attack?"

And my heart was thudding uncontrollably, as though it would burst right through my ribs. It raced even more wildly when Matt's arm tightened again as he gently drew me toward him. His face bent down to mine, and our lips met.

"Hold it right there! I see you!"

We sprang apart, staring up the rocks. The shout had been Tony's. In a moment I realized he wasn't speaking to us at all, but to Elise. But the mood between Matt and me had been shattered. There were voices all around us. Bubbles of laughter arose and burst on the wind.

From down by the campsite Mary Kay called, "What's going on? Is everybody OK?" And Phyllis and Corinna were up now, their flashlight beams washing over the rocks to reveal us all.

Yet as we clambered down again, all talking at once, I wondered what was happening to me. My heart had never pounded this way when I was with Bruce. One moment I felt so happy it was almost unbearable, the next I was overcome by doubt and a helpless yearning I had never known before.

And the cause of all my crazy jumbled feelings was Matt Jordan.

Chapter Eleven

"Mary Kay was telling me during break that the hostel where we'll stay is really spectacular." Matt had slowed down at a curve in the road to let me catch up with him. "I couldn't get her to describe it, though. She said it's a surprise."

"Well, we'll see it soon enough then." As always I felt tense when Matt was nearby, and the ordinary words of casual conversation got stuck somewhere in my throat. For nearly a week now we had been traveling along in the same bicycle caravan as if that moment on the rocky plateau had never been. Matt laughed and smiled with me, but I watched him closely enough to know that he laughed and smiled with everyone else, too. Sometimes, as now, he made a point of riding beside me. But other times he pedaled beside Elise or simply forged on ahead by himself, intent upon the scenery or lost in some reverie none of us could penetrate.

"You don't sound very enthusiastic," he said, studying my face. "You're usually so curious. What's the matter?"

"Nothing's the matter," I said curtly. Who did he think he was, anyway, making me feel as though he really cared about me one minute, then acting like there had never been anything between us the next? He had had plenty of opportunities to talk to me alone since the night when we told ghost stories. But as we had explored San Isabel National Forest, celebrated the Fourth of July, and traveled from hostel to hostel, he seemed to make sure there were always other people around us. He could've come with me as I went to gather firewood or to haul water for cooking. But Matt always invented some other chore that kept us apart.

Now he said, "Something's on your mind."

"Maybe," I admitted. "But I don't feel like talking about it."

Matt's feet slowed on the pedals. He looked at me, concerned, almost beseechingly. My anger began to melt away. "It's nothing I did, is it?" he asked, his voice low and compelling. "I mean, you're not mad at me or anything?"

"No," I said quickly. "How could I be mad at you? It's just—oh, I don't know, I kind of—"

"Oh, wow! Look at this!"

From up ahead Tony's shout jarred me back to the road and our mysterious destination. Matt tossed me a fleeting, apologetic look and surged forward eagerly. When I caught up with the others at the next bend, I saw why everyone was so excited.

There before us, gleaming in the afternoon sun, rose a stone castle. A magnificent central tower was surrounded by smaller turrets. Stately marbled columns flanked the arching entryway. Could this be our hostel?

"I didn't want to describe this place to you ahead of time. I thought nobody'd believe it," said Mary Kay. "I was here last year, and it's still the same."

"It's a reproduction, I suppose," Calvin remarked. "Who built it, anyway?"

"The story the Monteros told me—they're the hostel parents here—is that it was built by an eccentric millionaire named Wilmot Fitzhugh around 1910," Mary Kay said. "He was traveling in Scotland, and he saw a castle, and he liked it so much he had plans drawn up so they could build him an exact replica over here."

A sturdy, dark-skinned man in his early sixties, who introduced himself as Mr. Montero, hailed us as our bicycles rolled over the plank bridge that spanned the castle's moat. This was a magical place. Anything could happen here. If I could ever get things straight between Matt and me, it could happen that night, in these enchanted towers from another time.

"You're the one in charge of this trip?" he asked, pointing to Mary Kay. "You're the third group in tonight."

"Rats!" I muttered.

Matt turned, startled. "It's more fun when there are new people around, don't you think?"

"I guess so." I knew it was selfish to want the whole castle to ourselves. Still, it would have been nice to spend a quiet, intimate evening without the distraction of a lot of noisy strangers.

Mr. Montero led the way up a flagstone walk, between the marble columns, and through the entrance. We rode into a wide, shady courtyard where he told us we could chain up our bikes. Could there be any more romantic place for Matt and me to spend an evening together? I wondered. He had sounded concerned about me back there on the road. I felt sure he wanted to break down whatever constraint had grown between us. Even with two other groups around us, the castle was big enough to provide some private little spot where we could be alone.

"This is our main gathering room." Mr. Montero ushered us into an echoing, high-ceilinged hall. The other groups had already taken it over. Someone was playing a transistor radio at one end, competing with the Police cassette someone had put on at the other end. A couple of girls giggled in a corner, while two boys arm wrestled in front of the fireplace.

But even the commotion couldn't detract from the magnificence of the room—the enormous fireplace with its sweeping mantelpiece and its hearth of polished stone, the massive oak table, the swaying brass chandeliers. And there were tapestries on the walls—intricately woven scenes of mountain hunters and racing hounds, of armored knights and ladies-in-waiting. That morning I had woken up in a tent, stiff from sleeping on the ground, that night I would sleep in a castle! I couldn't quite grasp it.

I turned to Matt, eager to share my excitement. "Could you ever have imagined a place like this?" I asked. "It's right out of a book."

"Yeah, it's really neat," Matt said, but he sounded oddly detached.

Mr. Montero went to the mantel and picked up a sheaf of envelopes. "There's mail for this group," he announced. "You're very popular people. I've got six letters and a postcard here."

"Who are they for?" Matt stepped toward him eagerly.

"Let's see." Mr. Montero put on a pair of glasses and read slowly. "Here are two for Tony Nacotti. And a letter for Calvin Dexter the Third! Well! That's quite a name, isn't it? And here's something for you, Mary Kay—a postcard from Nebraska."

He studied it for so long, I almost thought he was going to read it before he handed it to Mary Kay. Matt still waited, jingling the change in his pocket. "Oh, and here's another letter for you, Calvin. And a nice thick one for Matthew Jordon."

I couldn't see Matt's face as he took the letter and read the address, but he hurried off to sit in a little alcove near the door.

What letter could be so important to him? He acted as if he'd been thinking of nothing else for days. A vague doubt tugged at my mind, and I pushed it aside. But it persisted. And suddenly I felt certain who the letter was from. It was from Jenny—Jenny who was just a friend.

Mary Kay called for a cooking squad, and I was one of the first volunteers to follow her out to the kitchen. The kitchen decor matched that of the rest of the castle, but it had all the modern conveniences, including a dishwasher. I was waiting my turn at the sink to wash some lettuce before I realized that I hadn't gotten a letter from Bruce.

Normally I would have felt empty and abandoned to arrive at a hostel and find no mail waiting for me. But now I hardly cared that Bruce hadn't written. After all, the last time we had talked on the phone we had had little enough to say to each other. Maybe Bruce was so busy with Melissa Snow that he'd forgotten about me. I found the thought strangely reassuring. Suppose things did work out between Matt and me. If Bruce had found someone else, too, I'd be spared the agony of breaking up with him when I got back to Kankakee. Our parting could be friendly and simple.

The head of lettuce slipped through my hands and fell into the sink. What was I thinking of? How could I consider breaking up with Bruce? We'd been together since eighth grade. How could I face school alone? Who would I sit with in the cafeteria? Would Jack and Sally still be my friends, or would they side with Bruce against me?

But if Matt really cared for me, I wouldn't be alone. Even though he'd be far away, I would know that Matt and I were together. There would be phone calls and plenty of letters back and forth.

Right now Matt was lost in a letter of his own. Had I only imagined the concern on his face this afternoon, the unspoken message that he wanted to be closer to me? And that night on the rocky plateau when his arms slipped around me and his face bent to mine—maybe that had all been part of his practical joke!

I hardly tasted the supper Phyllis and I threw together. Afterward I wandered out to the great hall, watching Matt from a distance. I hoped he would come sit beside me and suggest that we go exploring by ourselves. We would turn down narrow passageways, open a tiny door, and step into a secret walled garden where we could sit on a stone bench and pour out our deepest feelings for each other.

Two of the new girls had begun to play a recorder duet. On any other night I would have been happy just to listen, letting their melodies lead my imagination far from the everyday world. But now Matt blotted out everything else. He'd joined the ring of admirers around them. He seemed not to notice Elise as she gazed at him from a little round stool by the fireplace. He was completely absorbed in the music, as though nothing else existed.

I settled onto a little braided rug near his chair

and pretended that I was listening, too. Elise hitched her stool a little closer, but Matt was still lost in his own world. She shifted impatiently, but nothing she did captured his attention.

Corinna hovered for a few minutes at the edge of the group, looking bored, and finally slipped away alone. A little while later Phyllis and Calvin left the hall by a door at the far end. If only the music would come to an end, if only Matt could break free of his reverie and see me sitting beside him.

But the girls played on. Whenever one of their songs ended and I began to hope that they would put their instruments away, they whispered and giggled and selected still another tune.

"Elise," Tony called in one of their brief breaks. "You've got to come see this neat room full of old suits of armor!"

Elise threw a defiant look in Matt's direction as she rose from the stool. "Sure," she said. "I may as well."

For a moment Matt looked after her, but he made no move to call her back. Instead he reached into his pocket and drew out an envelope. He removed the letter, turned to the last page, and pored over it for several seconds before he put it into his pocket again.

Again the music stopped, and at last one of the girls began to take her recorder apart and put the pieces into a felt bag. "Hey, you're really great," Matt told them. "Don't quit already."

"We just want to take a break and look around a bit," said one of the girls. "We can play later if you want."

I had to say something to him now, before they urged him to go exploring with them. But there was only one question in my mind, and I had asked him about Jenny once already.

And as I sat there, searching desperately for a way to begin, he turned and smiled at me. "You're so quiet," he said in the same low, compelling voice I had heard on the road that afternoon. "Still have something on your mind?"

I was never any good at holding things back from him. "That must be an interesting letter you got," I said. "I bet I can guess who it was from."

I had tried to keep my tone light, but Matt gave me one of his keen, piercing looks just the same. "OK," he said, "who?"

"Jenny."

"Well, you're right. How'd you know?"

"Just from the way you were acting," I said. And against my better judgment I added, "Is she really just an old friend?"

"She fills me in on all the news from back home," he said.

136

He hadn't quite answered my question, but somehow I didn't want to ask it again.

"Hey, I'm going to get my guitar, maybe play some music when those girls come back, if you want to stick around," Matt said.

"No, thanks. I think I want to explore a little."

Why didn't he want to come with me? We could have roamed around the castle together, oblivious to everyone else.

I left the hall by a side door. I wandered aimlessly across a courtyard, up a narrow flight of steps, and into a little round turret room. Corinna was there alone, gazing at the full-length portrait of a bearded old gentleman in turn-of-the-century dress. I was almost beside her before she turned and smiled at me.

"I bet that's Wilmot Fitzhugh, the one who built this place," I said. Though I'd known her all these weeks, there were still moments when I forgot that she couldn't hear.

She took a slip of paper from her note pad and handed it to me with a questioning look. My comment hardly seemed worth repeating, but I wrote it down just to be polite.

Corinna looked back at the picture and nodded. Then she scribbled a message and handed it to me. "Wish I could show this place to Carlos."

"Who's Carlos?" I asked as she watched my face.

She wrote swiftly. "He goes to my school. He loves all this stuff—knights, armor, King Arthur stories."

"That's who you get letters from?" I wrote on the other side of her note.

She grinned as she wrote her reply. "Crazy letters. How about that guy who writes you?"

I hesitated, my pencil stub poised. "Bruce doesn't write much anymore," I wrote at last. After a moment I added, "Neither do I."

She nodded knowingly. She thought for a moment, then wrote another message. "Matt got a letter today, too. It even took his mind off Elise. Maybe now is your chance."

"Oh, come on!" I exclaimed. But Corinna just giggled. "He's got a girl back home," I wrote. "It's no use."

Corinna eyed me quizzically. "That girl's back home," she wrote. "You're right here."

What made Corinna think I had a chance with Matt? Somehow she had been imagining us together ever since the beginning of the trip, since that day at Bandelier when she'd trapped us in the cave. It had become remarkably easy to talk to her. Her written thoughts and the expressions on her face said as much as spoken words.

But somehow I couldn't put any more questions about Matt down on paper.

I looked down at the crumpled slips in my hand. Here was our entire conversation, back and forth, for anyone to read. Suppose Elise picked up one of our notes from the floor? What if Matt found them and read about my discouragement over his friend in Seattle?

"I better destroy the evidence," I wrote and took even that final message back from Corinna. No one else would ever know. Before we left the turret room, I tore up all of the notes and let them sift like snowflakes into a metal wastebasket that seemed oddly out of place in a castle.

Chapter Twelve

We stayed Friday night at a hostel outside the little town of Silver Plume. It had once been the dormitory of a girls' boarding school, and we were surrounded by characterless cinder-block walls and linoleum floors. There wasn't even anything memorable about the view. After the castle it was a big letdown.

Ours was the only group staying there that night, so we didn't even have the diversion of meeting new people. After supper we just sat around in the lounge with its plastic plants, looking at one another as though we had all run out of things to say.

"This is the home stretch," said Mary Kay, trying to stir up a spark of life. "We don't have another hostel between here and Boulder."

Elise moaned, "A solid week of camping? My hair's going to get so dirty it'll fall out."

"We're going to go through some landscapes that are more spectacular than anything you've seen yet," Mary Kay assured us. "Anyway, it's not a week, it's only four days. We get into Boulder next Tuesday night."

"Four days!" I exclaimed. I had less than a week to learn where I really stood with Matt. And somehow within the next four days I had to decide what to say to Bruce when I saw him again.

Maybe Bruce was the boy I really needed. At least he was solid and dependable, someone I'd always be able to count on, even if he was a little dull. That was the trouble, though. In spite of all his good points, Bruce just wasn't very exciting. He'd be happy to spend the rest of his life right in Kankakee. He'd go on working in his father's hardware store until he took over the business himself someday. Year after year he'd see the same crowd of friends, and they'd go bowling together or shoot pool or play Ping-Pong. And if he journeyed to Chicago some weekend to get a glimpse of the big city, he wouldn't be impressed at all. He'd just be relieved to get back home, to slide into his old routine again. Bruce never reached out to grab hold of new experiences. Had I really been that way myself?

"Matt, why don't you play us something?" Mary Kay suggested, still determined to lighten the mood.

I'd never known Matt to be reluctant to play, but that night he said, "Oh, I don't really feel like it." Something was bothering him. If only I could get him to tell me what it was. I'd show him I was the most patient, most understanding listener he could ever hope to find.

"Oh, come on," Elise insisted. "Just a couple of songs. What else is there to do between now and lights out?"

Reluctantly Matt got the guitar out of its case. His fingers slid over the strings, producing a series of random chords that failed to become a melody.

"How about a touch of the macabre," suggested Calvin. "Remember that one you taught us when we told ghost stories? 'Rickety Tickety Tin'?"

Matt nodded, but his singing didn't have its usual luster as he began: " 'Of a fair young maid I'll sing you a song, sing rickety tickety tin, of a fair young maid I'll sing you a song, she did not have her family long . . .' "

At first there was only a chuckle or two. Then

Elise and Calvin joined in on some of the repeated lines. Matt's voice gained strength, and by the time he reached the verse where "she threw her brother into the creek, the water tasted bad for a week . . ." I was singing and laughing, too.

Matt sang three or four more of his funny songs before he lapsed into a mellow mood. "I haven't played this one in a while," he said, rippling the strings. "It's the one I wrote a few weeks ago."

Then, very smoothly, he slid into the song I'd never forgotten:

"Your comings and your goings and your
    little turns of mind,
I see them every day and never wonder.
There are times I just don't see you,
    till those moments when I find
That the thought of you can shake my
    soul like thunder."

It seemed so long ago now, that night when I tried to read *Little Dorrit,* when I almost went for a walk with that shaggy-haired David from the marathon group. Elise had sat close beside Matt that night, hanging on every note he sang, and I had never doubted that she was the special someone who'd been on his mind lately.

But that night Elise sat on a stiff, vinyl-covered sofa with Tony. And when Matt began the final stanza he looked over at me.

"So I think I'm gonna tell you just how
    much I really care,
That I'll be with you when the road gets
    steep and narrow,
Yes, I really want to tell you there's
    a lot that we can share,
And I think I'm gonna say it all
    tomorrow."

Matt's voice paused, but his hands still drew the melody from the strings. And I knew I wasn't imagining things when his eyes locked with mine as he repeated the final line: "And I think I'm gonna say it all tomorrow."

" 'For purple mountains' majesty.' " The words slipped out before I could stop them, and I glanced around self-consciously, hoping no one had heard me.

But Matt was standing beside his bike just a few yards behind me. I blushed as his gaze met mine. "This has to be what the song is about," he said. "The only word to describe these mountains is *majestic*."

The peaks had been drawing nearer all day. It

would be impossible for me to capture the subtle hues of the mountains in a painting, the way they turned from green to blue to purple in the distance. I could only stand and gaze in awe.

"We sure picked the right place to spend our last free day," Calvin said in a rare moment of pure praise. "I can't imagine anything more beautiful than this."

"I'll show you the map I got at the ranger's office, so you can figure out where you want to go tomorrow," Mary Kay said. "It's got all the trails marked according to how easy or difficult they are, plus lots of warnings about where flash floods are likely to occur."

"They have avalanches around here every spring," said Matt. "I've read about skiers and climbers who've been trapped and even killed."

He had drawn his bike up right beside mine, and his comment was directed more to me than to anyone else. There had been moments like that all day, times when he turned to me with whatever he wanted to say as he had back in the beginning of the trip. We were definitely friends again, but were we anything more?

Matt's song had promised, "I think I'm gonna say it all tomorrow." All day I had waited, thrilling with anticipation each time a chance arose for us to talk alone. But nothing happened. Matt joked about the way Calvin always claimed it was beginner's luck whenever Phyllis beat him at chess. But the special words I dreamed of still hadn't come.

Our bicycle trip was gliding toward its inevitable close. It was Saturday night. The next day was our last free one for hiking and exploring. Monday and Tuesday we would bicycle all day to reach our final destination, the youth hostel outside Boulder. We had a free day there, Wednesday, but we would be caught up in the bustle of the city. Somehow in Boulder the group wouldn't be quite the same.

I couldn't bear waiting any longer. Somehow, in the days that remained to me, I would have to take matters into my own hands. I couldn't go back to Kankakee without knowing how Matt really felt about me. I would have to make something happen.

Mary Kay gave us a final briefing as we studied the park map after breakfast the next morning. "If anybody's interested, you can rent canoes back at the ranger's office. If you want to hike, I think the best trails are these." She traced two or three winding lines as I peered over her shoulder. "There's one canyon with a lot of petrified wood you can pick right off the ground," she went on. "And there's supposed to be a place along one of these little streams where the acoustics are really incredible." She paused, remembering. "They call it Echo Chasm. A friend of mine and I looked for it when we were here two years ago, but we never did find it."

"I wonder who her friend was?" Elise whispered. "I bet it was a guy."

But I was hardly listening; I was studying Matt, trying to decide the best way to approach him as he pored over the outspread map.

The others began to scatter. Tony and Elise left first, Tony determined to scale the most challenging of the surrounding peaks. Calvin and Phyllis headed off to look for the fossil canyon, Calvin talking and gesturing as usual while Phyllis kept her thoughts to herself. The others seemed interested in canoeing.

Mary Kay glanced over at me, and I knew that in another moment she'd invite me to join them. But I had other plans. And if I wanted to carry them out, I had to act now.

Quietly I stepped to Matt's side. "I think I'm going to look for Echo Chasm that Mary Kay was talking about," I said. "You want to come with me?"

The only reason I found the courage to speak was that I didn't give myself time to think. But the instant the words were out of my mouth I was swept with remorse. I had really pushed him too far this time. I should have been more

148

patient, let him approach me first. I'd probably ruined everything.

But when Matt turned, he didn't even look startled. "Sure," he said. "I had the same idea. From what I can figure out, we ought to take the trail that starts over there by that big ponderosa pine. It looks like it's about a five-mile trek, but we'll make it."

"Matt, Rhonda, don't you want to go canoeing?" Mary Kay called.

With a glow of satisfaction I heard Matt answer, "No, Rhonda and I are going for a hike."

The trail was smooth and easy to follow at first, although it was somewhat steep. In some places it was even wide enough for us to walk abreast. But after my first daring burst of words, I couldn't think of much worth saying, and most of the time we climbed in silence.

The path narrowed as we left the campsite farther behind. Matt led the way, now and then holding aside a branch or a thorny bush to let me pass more easily. I was starting to get out of breath, but I was afraid Matt might regret coming with me if I asked to stop and rest. Doggedly I forced my feet to plod on.

The sun was high in the sky when we heard running water up ahead. "Could we be there already?" I asked, trying to hide my disappointment. I might be tired, but I didn't want our hike together to end so soon.

"I don't think so." Matt peered up the trail around a boulder. "No, it's just a little creek."

The foundation of a footbridge was still visible, but the bridge itself was gone without a trace. The only way to cross the creek was by means of a ragged chain of stepping-stones.

"You make it look so easy," I said as Matt walked effortlessly from one jutting rock to the next.

He grinned back at me from the far bank, holding out his hand. "Come on," he called. "There's nothing to it."

The first two stones were placed close together, and I stepped lightly from one to the next. But the third stone was narrow and pointed, and I'd have to take an extra long stride to reach it.

Taking a deep breath, I stepped wide over the water. For half a second the rock was solid beneath my foot. Then it shifted, it bucked, and icy water swirled into my sneaker and up my calf.

"Watch out!" Matt yelled just an instant too late.

"Oh, no!" I groaned. Matt grabbed my hand and helped me clamber ashore. I laughed, a bit embarrassed.

"Is it very cold?" he asked, sounding really concerned.

"Not really. You could say it's refreshingly cool."

"Sure." Even though my rescue was complete, Matt still hadn't let go of my hand.

"No, really," I insisted. "I'm fine." I wasn't embarrassed anymore. We began to climb again, our clasped hands a link between us.

We were still quiet, but I no longer felt the strain of hunting for things to say. With Matt beside me it was a pleasure to climb the worn, uneven stairway that had been carved into a rock face, or to pause together beneath the proud, sweeping arms of a ponderosa pine, gazing down into the valley.

Suddenly Matt's hand tightened on mine. Wordlessly he lifted his free hand and pointed off to the left, to a little clump of bushes.

For a moment I didn't see why he was so excited. Then bushes waved, a leafy branch shuddered, and I saw it, too. A deer stood before us, its head high and alert, its broad twitching ears hungry for every sound.

For one hypnotic moment the deer held its pose, studying us intently, its nostrils quivering. Then, as though it had come to a sudden decision, it bounded away down the rocks. In another second it was lost to view.

"Wow!" Matt exclaimed. "I wish I'd had a camera. I guess it was a doe, it didn't have antlers."

"Oh, look!" This time I spotted it first. There was another stir in the thicket, and a second, smaller deer burst from the brush and leaped after the first. It never even turned its head in our direction. I only heard the snap of a dry twig and saw a blur of brown, a darting shape that was gone almost before I knew I had seen it at all.

"They sure can move!" Matt said. "Imagine being able to run like that."

"I wouldn't need stepping-stones to cross the creek," I said. "I'd go over it in one broad jump."

Matt gazed after the deer a moment longer. "Well, let's keep going," he said at last. "Echo Chasm can't be much farther now."

I didn't really care if we found it or not. That day would be with me forever. The scent of pine needles as we crushed them underfoot, the croaking cry of a raven, even the clamminess of my right sneaker took on a certain magic. I wanted to wander all day over these wild, winding trails, and it didn't matter where we went, as long as we were together.

When we hauled ourselves up one more jagged crest of rock onto a wide, windy plateau, I collapsed, winded. I let the wind whip my hair back from my face as I caught my breath. Matt, too excited to rest, went on ahead, "to get the lay of the land" as he put it. He was gone three or four minutes, and I was just beginning to wish I had gone with him when he dashed back, waving and shouting, "This is it! We found it! We found it!"

"Echo Chasm?" I was on my feet, rushing to meet him.

"You've got to hear it!" Matt cried. "It's incredible!"

We crossed the plateau and climbed a stony ridge. I heard tumbling water as we reached the top and looked down to discover a churning stream, which cut its way through a deep cleft in the mountainside.

"Hello!" Matt called. His voice had an eerie, hollow ring thrown against the chasm's walls. *Hello, lo, lo.* It bounced back from every side.

"We're here!" I hurled my own voice out over the stream and listened in delight as it came back again and again: *We're here, here, here . . . .*

"You want to try singing?" Matt asked. We both giggled as his words ricocheted from one wall to the other: *Try singing, singing, ing, ing, ing. . . .*

"Sure," I said. "Let's try 'Row, Row, Row Your Boat.' "

Matt held his hand like a conductor and signaled for us to begin. In unison we sang, " 'Row,

row, row your boat gently down the stream . . .' "
It was as if the voices of a dozen unseen singers,
hidden in crevices up and down the ravine, had
joined us.

Matt's face shone with excitement. "Let's try it
as a round this time," he said. "You come in on
boat."

"And who knows where *they'll* come in," I
said, giggling. Even the lightest flutter of laughter came whispering back, as if the mountain
wanted to share our mirth.

Matt began softly, and I joined him like an
echo myself. And trailing behind us, playing all
around our melody, shadows of our voices
chanted over and over: *Merrily, merrily, merrily,
merrily, life is but a dream, dream, dream,
dream . . .*

Slowly the last trembling echoes died away.
Once more there was only the gurgle of the
stream below us.

"This is one of the most amazing places I've
ever been," Matt said. "And it sure is nice being
here with you."

My mind reeled beneath the impact of his
words, and my heart began a wild drumming
accompaniment as the echoes whispered: *You,
you, you, you . . .*

Matt rested his hands on my shoulders, looking intently into my face. "I really mean it," he

said. "I love the way you get excited about things. You're not like any other girl I know."

Then, before I knew what was about to happen, Matt's arms folded around me, pressing me to him. "Rhonda," he murmured against my hair, so softly that the echoes could not mimic him. "You really are somebody special."

I closed my eyes as his lips met mine. I melted against the strength of his body, clinging to him as if I could make this moment last forever.

But almost as soon as I understand that what I'd wanted for so long had happened, Matt gently set me free. "Well," he said, and there was no mistaking the tenderness in his voice, "this is turning out to be a pretty wonderful day, isn't it?"

"It sure is." I sighed. Once there had been so much I wanted to say to him, but no longer. Words weren't really important anymore. What counted was touching, understanding, caring.

But Matt hadn't quite put words aside yet. "I've got to watch what I say," he said, laughing, and the echoes teased: *Say, say, say, say . . .* They were always there, even though sometimes I didn't notice them. "It feels like people are listening in on us, even way out here."

"It reminds me a little of exchanging notes with Corinna," I said. "It's that feeling you get that your words go on existing after you're all through with them."

Words got in the way sometimes, I thought. For now I didn't want to speak; I only wanted to drift silently through the rest of the day, and the next day and the day after that, through all the time that was still left to us, always with Matt beside me.

Chapter Thirteen

Dear Bruce,

  It's hard to know how to tell you this. I guess the summer has given me a lot of time to think. Maybe it's been that way for you, too. Anyway, I've begun to realize that . . . .

I stopped and chewed the end of my pen. How could I explain to Bruce that I'd met someone so much more exciting than he was? I should have written this letter weeks ago so he'd have had time to get over it before I got home. But back then I hadn't felt sure of Matt, the way I did now.

Writing my thoughts down might help me get them straight, but there wasn't time now for a letter to reach Bruce before I got back to Kankakee. I'd have to tell him some other way. Over the phone, maybe, or—I shuddered at the thought—face to face.

And after all, I reminded myself, Bruce might be with someone else by now, too. He might even be relieved when I told him I didn't want to go steady anymore. It felt strange, admitting to myself that Mom had been right all along. I *had* needed this summer away from home. If I'd never gone on the bicycle trip, I would never have seen the plaza in Santa Fe, the Rocky Mountains, or Echo Chasm. And I would never have met Matt Jordon.

I folded the letter and tucked it into my pocket as Matt hurried toward me. By the time I was on my feet, every thought of Bruce had fled from my mind.

"Since this is our last night of camping out," Matt said, "do you want to watch the sunset with me? We'll have a real good view up there." He pointed at the bald, rocky slope.

"Sure!" I exclaimed.

The memory of the day before and our magical hike still glowed, fresh and vibrant as the wild flowers Matt had picked for me that afternoon. And we had been creating new memories together all day—feeding bread crumbs to a chipmunk at breakfast, wandering off during our lunch break to explore a dried creek bed and nearly missing lunch. And we were always laughing about things that wouldn't really have been funny any other time. But that day, with Matt, laughing was one more way of being together as we rode along on our bikes.

"You guys be good now," Tony called to our backs as we headed out of camp. We giggled, and I stored that memory, too, to be cherished along with the rest. When I was back in Kankakee and Matt was thousands of miles away in Seattle, I would take out each detail and relive it again.

Of course, this wasn't really the end. We'd have to arrange to see each other again. Over Christmas vacation Matt could come to Kankakee—but he'd probably find it pretty boring. Maybe instead he'd invite me to Seattle. Seattle was beautiful, he'd been telling me, with its lake and its farmers' market and blackberries growing wild even in the parking lots.

"We can sit up here." Matt brushed the dust and dry twigs from a high, flat-topped rock. It was easily wide enough for both of us, and we sat a little apart, but close enough that our hands would be able to touch when the right moment came. The sun had sunk low in the western sky, but its light was still strong. Sunset wouldn't happen for a while yet, and I was glad for the chance to talk to Matt alone, free from the chatter and bustle of the rest of the group.

But for now we didn't talk much. Matt leaned back, supporting his weight on his hands, and we watched a little brown bird pecking among the pine needles not far from our feet. It was Matt who spoke at last, his voice so low the bird was not even startled. "You know, of all the girls in this group, you're the one I wish I'd spent more time with. Phyllis is so wound up with Calvin, and I don't know how much Corinna and I would have to say to each other even if I could learn sign language. And Elise—her helpless act can get a little tiresome after a while. But you're so open to things. I just love watching you look around. You look as if you're seeing everything for the first time."

Greedily I drank in his words. They would hold me over through that endless blank space that stretched ahead from the moment I boarded the plane Thursday afternoon.

"Elise has gotten better, but she never seems satisfied with anything," Matt went on. "She reminds me of Jenny sometimes. But Jenny's problem is that she always wants to analyze things when I wish she'd just leave them alone. I wish she could be a little more like you in some ways."

"Jenny?" I meant to say her name in a normal tone of voice, but somehow it came out a little unsteadily.

"Yeah," Matt said. "You know, the one whose name was in the book. You asked me about her once or twice."

"Sure," I said. "I remember." She was just a friend. There was no reason for my stomach to knot up this way just because he mentioned an old friend from back home. "Have you been writing to each other a lot?" I asked.

"I've only had two letters from her this whole trip," Matt said. "Every time we got to another hostel I thought there'd be a letter waiting from her. And then when there wasn't, I had to wait another two or three days till the next hostel."

The soft, wistful tone of his voice awakened a memory, a feeling I had almost forgotten. Once I had waited that way for Bruce's letters. Short as they were, each one had mattered so terribly much. But I hadn't guessed that Matt waited that way for letters from Jenny.

I couldn't find anything to say. Matt must have taken my silence to mean he should go on, because he continued, "When I started out on this trip, I never really thought I'd miss her. I figured we were getting too serious. We needed a break from each other so we could think things out."

I didn't want to know any of this. Still, some part of me made me ask, "And you do miss her? More than you expected to?"

"You'd better believe it," he said. "I figured this summer I'd get to know a lot of other girls and put this thing with Jenny in perspective. Only it hasn't worked out that way."

A jet plane ripped through the sky, its roar jarring the stillness of the mountainside. Maybe there was no such thing as real peace. Just when I thought all of my doubts about Matt had been put to rest, just when I'd been convinced I could count on him, my whole world had suddenly turned upside down.

"Matt," I said and stopped, struggling to put my thoughts in order. He gave me a long, searching look. I began again. "That song you wrote, that you said was for someone you'd been thinking of a lot—was it for her, Jenny?"

"Sure," he said. "Naturally."

I had already known what his answer would be, but it stung like a slap. I scrambled down from the rock.

"Where are you going?" Matt asked, startled. "Hey, what's the matter?"

"You're always so smart about reading my mind," I said. "You ought to be able to figure it out yourself." I couldn't bear to be alone with him any longer. I'd run back to camp to lose myself in the clatter of pots and arguments about whose turn it was to go for water.

"Rhonda, wait a second!" Now Matt was on his feet, too. He caught up with me when I had only gone three steps and put a restraining hand on my arm. "You're right, I should have figured it out. You're upset about Jenny. But really, you shouldn't—"

I jerked away from his touch. "You could have told me in the beginning! I asked you about her, and you made it sound like you didn't care about her at all."

"I didn't think I did. I was trying to keep her out of my thoughts. I didn't want to get all tied up with just one girl, I wanted to get to know a lot of different people—"

"You mean you wanted to lead us on," I broke in. "It wasn't just me, it was Elise, too. You'd get us interested in you, you'd treat each of us like we were important to you, and all the time you were writing songs about how wonderful you thought Jenny was."

"I wasn't trying to lead you on," Matt protested. "I thought with you of all people I wouldn't have any hassles because you had Bruce back home. All I wanted was to get to know you."

"But yesterday," I said, my voice thin and trembling. "The way you acted with me yesterday—it wasn't just because you wanted to get to know me. There *had* to be more to it than that."

"Yesterday was beautiful," Matt said. "Seeing those deer and singing rounds with the echoes—"

"But was that all? I thought—I thought it meant—"

Again Matt reached out to touch me, and this time I didn't have the strength to resist. Gently he held my hand between both of his. "No, it wasn't just the scenery," he said earnestly. "I really meant it when I said it was great sharing everything with you."

For an instant a fragile glimmer of hope made me lift my gaze to his face. But Matt wasn't finished speaking. "Yesterday was one of those special times that stands out, separate from everything else," he said. "But things like that don't last forever. You've got to appreciate them while you've got them and then move on."

"Just like that? Put it behind you like it didn't really count?"

"It counted, sure it counted. But it was just something that happened once. With Jenny it's different. We've known each other since we were freshmen, and we've been going together this whole past year. We don't even have to explain things to each other anymore. Half the time we just *know*. You know what I mean? You've probably got that kind of feeling with Bruce—"

"Oh, don't talk to me about him!" I pulled my hand free. And this time, even if he came running after me, I wouldn't turn around.

"Rhonda, don't!" Matt's voice was clear and commanding behind me.

Still I didn't turn, I didn't even try to glimpse the western sky that I knew was ablaze with color. I concentrated on keeping my footing as I stumbled along the rocky, twisting path back to camp, my legs shaking, my eyes clouded with tears.

Chapter Fourteen

For the last time I crammed my clothes into my saddlebags and stuffed my sleeping bag into the rattrap. For the last time I heard Mary Kay settle the debate about whose turn it was to carry the pots and pans. She pointed to Elise, who surprised everyone by accepting without a word of complaint. I tried not to watch Matt wrestle his guitar case into place on top of his rattrap.

"We're off!" Tony cried. And our noisy, clattering caravan set out for Boulder.

I pedaled in a kind of daze at the tail end of the procession, barely keeping pace with Elise. The rocks and trees were only a passing blur, and I hardly looked up when Calvin shouted that the big, broad-winged bird circling above us was an eagle. Nothing around me mattered anymore.

Matt tried to talk to me when we stopped for a break in the middle of the afternoon. "It seems weird to see so many cars on the road, doesn't it?"

"Are there any more than usual?" I asked. "I hadn't even noticed." I wouldn't let him see the feelings he still stirred in me. I'd make him think I'd erased all my romantic dreams about him. And maybe somehow I could convince myself.

"Just count them." He pointed toward the stretch of road before us. A beige Volkswagen whizzed past, then a green Chevy station wagon and a battered old Ford followed in quick succession.

"It's because we're so close to the city. Denver's over that way and Boulder's up ahead," Matt went on. He seemed oblivious to the fact that I didn't want to talk. "Even taking these back roads, you start to see the traffic."

"I guess so."

"We'll have a view of Boulder from the hostel," Matt said. "It'll be funny, looking out at a city. After all these weeks on the road, I can almost believe the whole country's nothing but mountains and woods."

"Well, I can't," I said shortly. Why did he have

to persist in this artificial friendliness? In two days I'd never have to see him again. Couldn't he just leave me in peace now?

"Hey, I was thinking," Matt tried once more. "Maybe it'd be a nice idea if we took Mary Kay out for pizza tonight."

"Sure. Sounds like a good idea." Looking back, I had to admit Mary Kay had been a pretty good sport about the night we went swimming and the time the boys tried to scare us after we'd been telling ghost stories. That had been the first time I really let myself care about Matt. Before that I had tried hard to stay loyal to Bruce. But I didn't want to think about that now.

"Well, I'll go suggest it to the other guys," Matt said. "See how they feel about it. We can make it a surprise for her."

"OK," I said. At last he was going away and leaving me in peace. But I longed to call after him, *Matt, please come back, please. . . .*

As usual, Matt was right. I wasn't quite prepared for the onslaught of traffic leading to the city. But at five o'clock our quiet meandering road met an access highway to a major highway that was swarming with rush-hour cars and trucks. The hostel was in an area that had been rural until a dreary strip of fast-food joints, cheap motels, video arcades, and discount stores crept up around it. Without the mountains in the background, it would've looked just like the outskirts of Kankakee.

Mary Kay assured us that Boulder itself was a lovely city, especially around the university. Elise, Corinna, and Phyllis glowed with excitement. They couldn't wait to spend the next morning shopping, but I couldn't work up any enthusiasm for an excursion among the clothing racks. Maybe I'd lost the knack for civilization.

The hostel was a rambling old farmhouse, and just as Matt had said, we could see the city from the upstairs windows. Elise gazed out as though she were hypnotized. But I just dumped my gear onto a bed and sank down, too discouraged to move.

I wasn't allowed any peace, however. Corinna dropped down beside me within a minute, thrusting a note under my nose. "Go downstairs. See what Mary Kay just got."

"Later," I said, shaking my head. But now Elise joined us, eager to know what was going on, and Corinna acted so mysterious that even I began to feel curious. Without knowing quite why, I followed them down the creaking stairs to the living room.

Mary Kay stood with her back to the cold fireplace, her face flushed with happiness. In her right hand she held a lush bouquet of red roses.

"From her boyfriend, I bet," said Elise. And Mary Kay giggled and held out a card that had come with the flowers.

"He's congratulating me for steering you all safely to port," she said. "And he says he'll see me in New York! He just got a teaching job on Long Island."

We all crowded around to admire the flowers. Mary Kay reminded me of a princess in a fairy tale, standing there basking in the glow of our attention. For the first time all summer she wasn't just our group leader, announcing schedules and enforcing the rules of the hostels. Now she really did have a life of her own, a life that I could imagine and understand.

But Mary Kay's story had a happy ending.

I caught myself glancing at Matt. He stood by himself, studying the rack of tongs and pokers by the hearth. It wasn't often that he seemed lonely and detached from the group.

Well, simply because Matt looked a little pensive didn't mean he was harboring wistful thoughts about me. Probably he was just dreaming about his glorious reunion with Jenny back in Seattle.

Maybe the whole trip had been a trick I let my imagination play on me. I had never really changed. Sure, I'd glimpsed a world that was wider than Kankakee, that thrilled me at times. But what did that matter to someone like me? I knew where I really belonged: back with the people I'd known all my life. Kankakee held no surprises. But it couldn't disappoint me, either. And even if Bruce was rather boring at times, at least I knew what to expect from him.

For once I had a pocketful of change and didn't have to make the rounds borrowing nickels and dimes. Quietly, hoping Matt wouldn't guess where I was headed, I slipped out to the pay phone I had noticed in a hallway just off the kitchen. It was a good thing I hadn't sent Bruce a letter of farewell, I thought as the phone rang in Kankakee far away. He might have taken me seriously, when I'd only been carried away by a silly, childish daydream.

The phone rang three times before Bruce's father picked it up. "Hello?" he said.

"Hi," I said. "Is Bruce there? This is Rhonda."

"Uh, hold on a second." I heard Bruce's father lay the receiver down, and there was a murmur of distant voices before he came back on the line. "He's out right now, Rhonda. He told his mom he wouldn't be back till late."

Bruce had the trip schedule. He knew that I'd be near a phone that night and that I was bound to call him.

"Where'd he go?" I asked.

His father hesitated. "I'm not sure where they were going."

They? Who did he mean? "Oh," I said. "Well, thanks."

"Listen, I'll tell him you called, all right? He'll be sorry he missed you."

"OK," I said. "Bye."

Voices came from the living room—Calvin sounding forth on some minor point, Elise laughing coquettishly. I sat motionless on the chair by the phone. So Bruce hadn't spent the evening waiting by the phone for my call. He was out on the town, enjoying his last night of freedom before I came home.

Well, what right did I have to expect him to sit around waiting for me? I hadn't exactly given him my every waking thought these past weeks. And if I'd been spending this last evening with Matt, I wouldn't have spared one precious moment on a call to Bruce.

So why had I tried to call him? I hadn't really wanted to talk to him. Actually, I was almost relieved that he was out. I had only wanted to make sure that when I got home I wouldn't have to be alone.

But it wasn't going to work. After this trip, after knowing Matt, Bruce could never be the same to me again. Somehow I'd have to explain to him that my feelings toward him had changed. I would have to be alone for a while, maybe a long while, until I met someone else who was exciting and aware, someone who made me feel the way I had felt this summer with Matt Jordon.

"Come on, Matt. Get your guitar," Elise was urging as I went back into the living room. "It's our last night together."

"Maybe later." Matt still looked lost in thought as he sat in one corner of the couch, thumbing through an old issue of *Time* magazine.

Elise didn't seem too disappointed. She and Tony whispered and giggled in a corner. Mary Kay set her flowers in a vase on the coffee table. Calvin was telling Phyllis a long story about someone he knew who was a genius, and Phyllis gazed at his face with rapt attention.

Corinna caught my eye. She moved her hands in Matt's direction and lifted her eyebrows in a question. I shook my head. With no words at all, we managed to understand each other perfectly.

I could hardly remember my dismay that long-ago evening when I learned that two of the other girls on the trip were deaf. I had felt so isolated, so fearful of everything that was new and different. But all those miles on the road hadn't only strengthened my calf muscles, I had seen a slice of the world beyond Kankakee, Illinois, and I wanted to see more and more.

And these people I had traveled with were all part of my sense of discovery. Despite all their quirks, I had grown attached to each of them. The trip had given me something that even Matt couldn't take away.

I looked around the living room from one face to the next, and suddenly I had an overwhelming desire to preserve the whole scene forever. After that night I might never see any of these people again. I decided to sit at the edge of the circle and try to capture them all in a quick sketch, something I could work on later when I got home, something that would prove to me that the summer had been real.

As I dug through my saddlebag, hunting for my box of pencils, my hand closed over a battered paperback book. Slowly I drew it out and opened it to the title page. "To Matt," I read. "To let you know I'll be thinking of you this summer. Jenny."

She hadn't written "Love, Jenny." Just her name, simple and direct. Maybe she didn't want to frighten him away. Even though they'd been going together for a year, she had to choose her words carefully. Even Jenny hadn't been sure of him.

I went downstairs again, the book in one

hand, my sketch pad and pencils in the other. But my impulse to draw had begun to fade. Slowly, tentatively, I approached Matt and held out *The Milagro Beanfield War.*

"Here," I said. "I almost forgot to return this to you."

He grinned up at me. "Are you still talking to me?" he asked.

"I never said I wasn't," I protested.

"I know. You never *said* anything. That's what made me wonder if you were still talking to me." There was that familiar hint of mischief in his voice, but it soon disappeared. "Let's go out for a walk," he said seriously, glancing around the room. "This might be our last chance to really talk."

For a moment I felt a tremor of hope. He was going to tell me he had changed his mind. It *wasn't* Jenny he cared about, he realized now. It had been me all along.

But something in the look on his face, or perhaps the slow, deliberate way he got to his feet, warned me not to expect too much. And out on the road that led away from the front door he began, "You know, you're right. I guess I really did lead you on these past couple of weeks, and it wasn't fair."

"Why did you do it?" I burst out. "Didn't you ever stop to think how I might feel about you?"

Matt thrust his hands into his pockets. He kicked at a stone, and it skipped into the gutter. "I didn't think about it enough," he admitted, not quite meeting my gaze. "Mostly I was just thinking about myself. I kept telling myself I had to keep my options open, because that's what the summer was for. I thought everything would be fine as long as I didn't commit myself to anybody."

I couldn't remember ever hearing Matt criticize himself before. It made him seem oddly vulnerable. But I was still too hurt to reach out to him, to tell him it was really all right. "You like the attention," I said bitterly. "You really like having lots of girls hanging on your every word."

"I suppose that's a part of it," he admitted. "It does make a guy feel good, you know? But the worst part for me is having to make up my mind. Like—I look at Elise, and she's kind of charming really, the way she needs someone to do things for her. And you—you really *are* special, Rhonda, I wasn't just giving you a line. You've got such a fresh way of seeing things. Being with you could never get boring."

"You really mean that?"

Matt nodded his head. "All day I've wanted to tell you how much I really enjoyed getting to know you. You've made this whole trip a lot more fun for me. And I didn't ever mean to hurt you."

He said it so softly, so urgently, that I knew he meant it. "I think I'll live," I said with a little laugh. I had to let him know I was going to be all right, even if I still wasn't quite sure of that myself.

"Then I didn't make it an awful summer for you?" he asked, still searching for reassurance.

"No." I thought back over the past few weeks and all that we had done together. I remembered that first, lonely night in Santa Fe when Matt was the only person to whom I could talk. I remembered the time Corinna trapped us in the Anasazi cave and the night of the ghost stories. Most of all I remembered Echo Chasm. "No," I said again. "You've made it a fantastic summer."

For a while we walked along in silence. Crickets chirped away in the grass along the roadside. "I really did think we could just be friends, without any complications," Matt said at last. "I figured you wouldn't want to get involved with anybody new because you had somebody back home already."

"I thought that, too, in the beginning," I said. "Only I've started to see Bruce differently. I don't feel he's the kind of guy I want to spend a whole lot of time with anymore. We'd gotten to the point where we took each other for granted because we were together so much."

It was the first time I'd spoken these thoughts

178

aloud, though they had been taking form in my mind for weeks. "You know," I added after a moment, "I might not have figured any of that out if it hadn't been for you."

"I don't know if I should feel good about that or not," Matt said with a wry laugh. "I've done you the favor of getting you to break up with your boyfriend."

"I didn't mean it quite like that," I said, laughing a little myself. "I mean, if I'd really cared about Bruce as much as I thought I did, I couldn't have gotten hung up on somebody else, could I? And besides—" I paused, groping for just the right words. "Besides, being with you this summer, you showed me what I'd really like to find in a guy. I want somebody who's curious and gets excited about things. Somebody who doesn't feel he's already learned everything he ever wants to know."

"Maybe when you see each other, everything will go back to the way it used to be," Matt said.

I shook my head. "It can't," I told him. "I'm different now. The summer changed me too much."

And this was the biggest challenge of all, I reflected—the kind of challenge Mom had really meant me to face on this trip. I couldn't hide behind Bruce any longer. Challenges were scary, but they had a way of opening up the world.

The roar of the highway swelled up ahead. Our quiet evening walk was coming to an end. It was time to turn back.

We didn't have much to say on the walk back to the hostel, but there wasn't much need for words. Just before we reached the front drive Matt stopped, and when I turned to look at him, he caught me in a quick, laughing embrace. "I'm going to miss you," he said, letting me go. "I'm going to miss you a lot."

"Me, too," I said. "It's going to take me awhile."

But I didn't want to get somber again. I felt light and free in a way I hadn't felt in a long time. "Hey," I said, "we're taking Mary Kay out for pizza, aren't we?"

Matt nodded. "Come on, let's go in and break the news."

He grabbed my hand, and together we crossed up to the wooden porch, the best of friends.

Watch for Something Special
Coming from Sweet Dreams
in January 1985

STAR STRUCK!

by
Shannon Blair

It's the thrill of a lifetime when Carrie is cast as an extra in a rock video starring Michael Jackson! The work is a dream come true—there's even a romance with Joe, another extra. Things seem to be going great for Carrie, until her expectations get a little out of hand . . .

Buy STAR STRUCK! on sale January 15, 1985 wherever Bantam paperbacks are sold.

You'll fall in love with all the Sweet Dream romances. Reading these stories, you'll be reminded of yourself or of someone you know. There's Jennie, the *California Girl*, who becomes an outsider when her family moves to Texas. And Cindy, the *Little Sister*, who's afraid that Christine, the oldest in the family, will steal her new boyfriend. Don't miss any of the Sweet Dreams romances.

☐	24327	SECRET IDENTITY #22 Joanna Campbell	$2.25
☐	24407	FALLING IN LOVE AGAIN #23 Barbara Conklin	$2.25
☐	24329	THE TROUBLE WITH CHARLIE #24 Jaye Ellen	$2.25
☐	22543	HER SECRET SELF #25 Rhondi Villot	$1.95
☐	24292	IT MUST BE MAGIC #26 Marian Woodruff	$2.25
☐	22681	TOO YOUNG FOR LOVE #27 Gailanne Maravel	$1.95
☐	23053	TRUSTING HEARTS #28 Jocelyn Saal	$1.95
☐	24312	NEVER LOVE A COWBOY #29 Jesse Dukore	$2.25
☐	24293	LITTLE WHITE LIES #30 Lois I. Fisher	$2.25
☐	23189	TOO CLOSE FOR COMFORT #31 Debra Spector	$1.95
☐	24837	DAY DREAMER #32 Janet Quin-Harkin	$2.25
☐	23283	DEAR AMANDA #33 Rosemary Vernon	$1.95
☐	23287	COUNTRY GIRL #34 Melinda Pollowitz	$1.95
☐	24336	FORBIDDEN LOVE #35 Marian Woodruff	$2.25
☐	24338	SUMMER DREAMS #36 Barbara Conklin	$2.25
☐	23340	PORTRAIT OF LOVE #37 Jeanette Noble	$1.95
☐	24331	RUNNING MATES #38 Jocelyn Saal	$2.25
☐	24340	FIRST LOVE #39 Debra Spector	$2.25
☐	24315	SECRETS #40 Anna Aaron	$2.25
☐	24838	THE TRUTH ABOUT ME AND BOBBY V. #41 Janetta Johns	$2.25
☐	23532	THE PERFECT MATCH #42 Marian Woodruff	$1.95
☐	23533	TENDER-LOVING-CARE #43 Anne Park	$1.95
☐	23534	LONG DISTANCE LOVE #44 Jesse Dukore	$1.95
☐	24341	DREAM PROM #45 Margaret Burman	$2.25
☐	23697	ON THIN ICE #46 Jocelyn Saal	$1.95
☐	23743	TE AMO MEANS I LOVE YOU #47 Deborah Kent	$1.95

Prices and availability subject to change without notice.

SWEET VALLEY HIGH

☐	23969	**DOUBLE LOVE #1**	$2.25
☐	23971	**SECRETS #2**	$2.25
☐	23972	**PLAYING WITH FIRE #3**	$2.25
☐	23730	**POWER PLAY #4**	$2.25
☐	23943	**ALL NIGHT LONG #5**	$2.25
☐	23938	**DANGEROUS LOVE #6**	$2.25
☐	24001	**DEAR SISTER #7**	$2.25
☐	24045	**HEARTBREAKER #8**	$2.25
☐	24131	**RACING HEARTS #9**	$2.25
☐	25016	**WRONG KIND OF GIRL #10**	$2.50
☐	24252	**TOO GOOD TO BE TRUE #11**	$2.25
☐	24358	**WHEN LOVE DIES #12**	$2.25
☐	24524	**KIDNAPPED #13**	$2.25

<u>Prices and availability subject to change without notice.</u>

Buy them at your local bookstore or use this handy coupon for ordering:

Bantam Books, Inc., Dept SVH, 414 East Golf Road, Des Plaines, Ill. 60016

Please send me the books I have checked above. I am enclosing $_____ (please add $1.25 to cover postage and handling). Send check or money order —no cash or C.O.D.'s please.

Mr/Mrs/Miss _____

Address _____

City_____ State/Zip_____

SVH—1/85

Please allow four to six weeks for delivery. This offer expires 7/85.